Gabe accompanied the Sultan into a vast dining room, where lavishly laid tables were decorated with fragrant roses coloured deep crimson.

'I have seated you next to the Ambassador of Maraban, one of the most influential men in the region,' said the Sultan. 'With my sister on the other side. Her English is excellent and she is eager to meet with you. Ah, here she comes now. Leila!'

But Gabe didn't need to hear his host say her name to know the woman's identity. He knew that from the moment she entered the banqueting hall. Even though Leila's body was swathed in flowing silk, and even though a matching veil of palest silver was covering half her face, there could be no mistaking her. No amount of camouflage could disguise the sexy sway of her body—or maybe it was because in some primeval and physical way he still felt connected to her.

He could still smell her on his skin.

THE DESERT MEN OF QURHAH

Their destiny is the desert!

The heat of the desert is nothing compared to the passion
that burns between the pages of this stunning new trilogy
by Sharon Kendrick!

Defiant in the Desert
December 2013

Oil baron Suleiman Abd al-Aziz has been sent to
retrieve the Sultan of Qurhah's reluctant fiancée—
a woman who's utterly forbidden, but is determined to
escape the confines of her engagement…by seducing him!

Shamed in the Sands
February 2014

The Princess of Qurhah has always wanted
something different from her life. So when sexy
advertising magnate Gabe Steele arrives to work for
her brother, Leila convinces Gabe to give her a job…
but that's not the only thing to cause a royal scandal!

Seduced by the Sultan
April 2014

The Sultan of Qurhah is facing a scandal of
epic proportions. His fiancée has run off,
leaving him with a space in his king-sized bed.
A space once occupied by his mistress Catrin Thomas.
And now he wants her back—at any price!

SHAMED
IN THE SANDS

BY
SHARON KENDRICK

® and TM are trademarks owned and used by the trademark owner
and/or its licensee. Trademarks marked with ® are registered with the
United Kingdom Patent Office and/or the Office for Harmonisation in
the Internal Market and in other countries.

Published in Great Britain 2014
by Mills & Boon, an imprint of Harlequin (UK) Limited,
Eton House, 18-24 Paradise Road, Richmond, Surrey, TW9 1SR

© 2014 Sharon Kendrick

ISBN: 978 0 263 90823 7

Harlequin (UK) Limited's policy is to use papers that are natural,
renewable and recyclable products and made from wood grown in
sustainable forests. The logging and manufacturing processes conform
to the legal environmental regulations of the country of origin.

Printed and bound in Spain
by Blackprint CPI, Barcelona

Sharon Kendrick started storytelling at the age of eleven, and has never really stopped. She likes to write fast-paced, feel-good romances with heroes who are so sexy they'll make your toes curl!

Born in west London, she now lives in the beautiful city of Winchester—where she can see the cathedral from her window (but only if she stands on tiptoe!). She has two children, Celia and Patrick, and her passions include music, books, cooking and eating— and drifting off into wonderful daydreams while she works out new plots!

Recent titles by the same author:

DEFIANT IN THE DESERT
  (Desert Men of Qurhah)
THE GREEK'S MARRIAGE BARGAIN
A SCANDAL, A SECRET, A BABY
BACK IN THE HEADLINES
  (Scandal in the Spotlight)

**Did you know these are also available as eBooks?
Visit www.millsandboon.co.uk**

For Olly Wicken, whose imagination and expertise
helped bring Gabe to life. Thank you.

CHAPTER ONE

GABE STEEL WAS naked when he heard the sound of knocking.

He picked up a towel and scowled. He wanted peace. No, he *needed* peace. He'd come to this strange city for all kinds of reasons—but none of them included being disturbed when he had just stepped out of the shower.

He thought about the harsh light of spring he'd left behind in England. The way it could still make his heart clench with pain at this time of year. He thought how guilt never really left you, no matter how deeply you tried to bury it. If you scratched beneath the surface you could always bring up stuff you didn't want. Which was why he didn't scratch. Ever.

But sometimes you couldn't escape it, no matter how hard you tried. Hadn't one of the staff sent someone up earlier, asking if he would like any special arrangements made for his birthday? He'd wondered how the hell they had known it was his birthday— until he realised that they had seen his passport when he'd checked in yesterday.

He stood still and listened. The knocking had stopped and everything was quiet again. He started to slide the towel over one hair-roughened thigh when the sound resumed, more urgently this time.

At any other time and in any other place, he would have ignored the unwanted summons and carried on with what he was doing. But Gabe recognised that these were not normal circumstances. This job was a first. He'd never been the guest of a member of a royal family before. Correction. The *head* of a royal family. He'd never worked for a sultan before—a man who ruled over one of the world's wealthiest countries and who had already lavished on Gabe a breathtaking amount of hospitality. And maybe that was what was beginning to irritate him most of all—because he didn't like to be beholden to anyone, no matter how exalted their position.

Uttering a muttered curse beneath his breath, Gabe wrapped the towel around his hips and crossed a room so vast that back home the walk might almost have qualified as a workout. He'd stayed in some amazing places in his time, and his own place in London was pretty mouth-watering. But he had to acknowledge that this penthouse suite in Qurhah's finest hotel took luxury to a whole new level.

The knocking continued. A low drumming sound he found impossible to ignore—and its persistence made his impatience increase. He pulled open the door to find a woman standing there. Or rather, a woman who was doing her best not to look like a woman.

Tall and slim, her body was completely covered and her features were in shadow. She was carrying a briefcase and wearing a trench coat over a pair of jeans, with a fedora hat pulled down low over her face. Her appearance was so androgynous that she could almost have been mistaken for a man. But Gabe could smell a woman's scent in a pitch-black room, even when she wasn't wearing perfume. He could accurately assess the hip-width of a pair of panties from nothing more than a cursory glance. Where the opposite sex was concerned, he was an expert—even if his expertise went no further than the physical.

Because he didn't do *emotional*. He didn't need a woman to unpick his mind at the end of a stressful day, or cry on his shoulder in the mistaken belief that it might make his heart melt. And he certainly didn't want some unknown female turning up today, when his heart was dark and his schedule full.

'Where's the fire?' he demanded.

'Please.' Her voice was low and urgent and very faintly accented. 'Can I come in?'

His lips gave the faintest curve of contempt. 'I think you must have the wrong room, sweetheart,' he said and started to shut the door.

'Please,' she repeated—only this time he could hear panic underpinning her words. 'Men are trying to find me.'

It was a stark appeal and it stopped Gabe in his tracks. It wasn't the kind of thing he heard in the slick, controlled world he called his life. It took him back to a time and a place where threat was a constant. Where fear was never very far away.

He stared down at her face and he could see the wide gleam of alarm in eyes shadowed by the fedora.

'Please,' she said again.

He hesitated for no longer than a heartbeat before something kicked in. Some unwanted protective urge over which he seemed powerless. And he didn't do powerless.

'Come in,' he said abruptly. He caught the drift of her spicy perfume as she hurried past, and the fragrance seemed to cling to his skin as he closed the door and turned to face her. 'So what's the story?'

She was shaking her head and turning to look at the door as if she was petrified somebody was going to burst in behind her.

'Not now,' she said in that soft accent, which was making his senses start to prickle into life. 'There's no time. I'll tell you everything you need to know But only when it's safe. They mustn't find me here. They mustn't.'

She was looking at the far side of the vast room, where the open bedroom door revealed the unmade bed, on which he'd been taking a catnap before his shower. He saw her quickly turn her head away.

'Where can you hide me?' she questioned.

Gabe's eyes narrowed. He thought her attitude was arrogant—almost imperious—considering the way she'd burst in on him like this. He was the one doing *her* a favour—and a little gratitude wouldn't have gone amiss. But maybe now was not the time to give her a lecture on the etiquette of gate-crashing—not when she was looking so jittery.

He thought about where he used to hide whenever the bailiffs bashed on the door. The one room which always seemed safer than any other.

'Go through into the bathroom,' he said, flicking his fingers in the direction of the en-suite. 'Crawl underneath the tub and stay there until I tell you otherwise. And your explanation had better be good enough to warrant this unwanted intrusion into my time.'

But she didn't appear to be listening. She was already moving towards the bathroom with an unconscious sway of her slender bottom before she was lost to view.

And somehow she had managed to transfer her anxiety to Gabe and his body began to react accordingly. He could feel adrenalin coursing through his bloodstream and the sudden pounding of his heart. He wondered whether he should put on some clothes and then realised there was no time, because he could hear the heavy approach of footsteps in the corridor outside.

The rap on the door was loud and he opened it to find two men outside, their eyes as dark and pinched as raisins. Loose suits did little to conceal their burly strength, and Gabe could detect the telltale bulges of gun holsters packed against each of their bodies.

The taller of the two let his gaze flicker to Gabe's still-damp torso and then to the small towel which was knotted at his hip. 'We are sorry to disturb you, Mr Steel.'

'No problem,' said Gabe pleasantly, registering that they knew his name, just as everyone else in the hotel seemed to. And that their accents sounded like a pronounced version of the one used by the mystery woman currently cowering in his bathroom. 'What can I do for you?'

The man's accent was thick. 'We are looking for a woman.'

'Aren't we all?' questioned Gabe conspiratorially, with a silken stab at humour. But neither man took the bait and neither did they respond to the joke. Their faces remained unsmiling as they stared at him.

'Have you seen her?'

'Depends what she looks like,' said Gabe.

'Tall. Early twenties. Dark hair,' said the smaller of the two men. 'A very…striking woman.'

Gabe gestured towards the tiny towel at his hips and rubbed his hands over his upper arms, miming a chill which wasn't quite fictitious, since the icy kick of the air-conditioning was giving him goose-bumps. 'As you can see—I've been taking a shower. And I can assure you that nobody was keeping me company at the time—more's the pity.' He glanced over his shoulder towards the room before turning back to them, his forced smile hinting at a growing irritation. 'Of course, you're perfectly at liberty to look for yourselves, but I'd appreciate it if you could do it swiftly. I still have to get dressed and shaved—and I'm due to dine with the Sultan in a couple of hours.'

It worked. The mere mention of the Sultan's name produced the reaction he'd hoped for. Gabe thought it almost comical as he watched both men take a step back in perfect unison.

'Of course. Forgive us for interrupting you. We will take up no more of your time, Mr Steel. Thank you for your help.'

'My pleasure,' said Gabe, and closed the door softly behind them.

His footsteps across the carpet were equally soft, and when he opened the bathroom door, the woman was just slithering out from under the bathtub like some kind of sexy serpent. He felt the instant rush of heat to his groin as she scrambled to her feet and began brushing her hands over her body.

The fedora had fallen off and as she raised her face and he got a proper look at her for the first time he felt awareness icing his skin. Because suddenly he was looking at the most arresting woman he had ever seen. His mouth dried with lust. She looked like a fantasy come to life. Like a character from the *Arabian Nights* who had wandered into his hotel bathroom by mistake.

Her olive skin was luminous and her dark-fringed eyes were a bright shade of blue. A ponytail of black hair hung almost to her waist—hair so shiny that it looked as if she might have spent the morning polishing it. Despite the silky trench coat, he could see that her breasts were neat and her legs so long that she would have been at home on any international catwalk.

Her face remained impassive as he looked her over, as if she was no stranger to submission. Only the faintest flush of pink in her cheeks gave any indication that she might be finding his attention unsettling. But what did she expect? If you burst into a strange man's bedroom and demanded refuge, then surely the normal rules of conduct flew right out of the window.

'They've gone,' he said shortly.

'So I heard.' She hesitated. 'Thank you.'

He noticed the way her gaze kept flickering towards his bare torso and then away again. As if she knew she shouldn't stare at him but couldn't help herself. He gave a grim kind of smile. It wasn't the first time he had encountered such a problem.

'I think you owe me an explanation,' he said. 'Don't you?'

'Sure.' She bent to pick up her briefcase, and as she

straightened up she did that not-quite-looking thing at his chest again. 'Just not...not in here.'

Was the intimacy of the setting too much for her? he wondered. Was she aware that beneath the tiny towel his body was beginning to respond to her in a way which might make itself embarrassingly obvious if he wasn't careful? He could feel the hot pump of arousal at his groin and suddenly he felt curiously vulnerable.

'Go through there,' he said abruptly. 'While I get dressed.'

The stir of his erection had subsided by the time he'd pulled on some jeans and a T-shirt and walked through to the sitting room to see her standing with her back to him. She was staring out of the panoramic windows which overlooked the city of Simdahab, where golden minarets and towers gleamed in the rich light of the late afternoon sun. But Gabe barely noticed the magnificent view—his attention remained captivated by the mystery stranger.

She had removed her trench coat and had slung it over the back of one of the sofas—was she planning on staying?—and suddenly there were no more concealing folds to hide her from his eyes. His gaze travelled to where denim clung to the high curves of her bottom, to where her dark ponytail hung down her back like a dark stream of satin.

She must have sensed that he was in the room because she turned round—the ponytail swinging in slow motion—and from this angle he thought the view was even better. She looked at him with those clear blue eyes, and suddenly all he could see was temptation.

He wondered if she had been sent to him by the

Sultan—a delicious package for him to open and enjoy at his leisure. Another lavish gift, just like the others which had been arriving at his hotel suite all morning. It was said that, despite his relative youth, the Sultan was an old-fashioned man and this might be a very old-fashioned gesture on his part. Mightn't the powerful potentate have decided to sweeten up Gabe with a woman? A submissive and beautiful woman who would cater to his every whim…

'Who are you?' he questioned coolly. 'A hooker?'

Her face showed no reaction to his crude question, but it seemed to take for ever before she spoke.

'No, I'm not a hooker. My name is Leila,' she said, and now her blue eyes were watchful.

'Pretty name, but I'm still no wiser.'

'Mr Steel—'

Gabe shook his head in faint disbelief. 'How come everyone in this city knows my name?'

The woman smiled—her lips softening into cushioned and rosy curves. And even though he had never paid for sex in his life, in that moment he almost wished she *were* a hooker. What would he get her to do first? he wondered. Unzip him and take him in her delicious mouth, and suck him until he came? Or lower those narrow hips and bounce around on him until he cried out with pleasure?

'People know who you are because you are the guest of the Sultan,' she was saying. 'Your name is Gabe Steel and you are an advertising genius who has come to Qurhah to improve our global image.'

'That's a very flattering summary,' offered Gabe drily. 'But I'm afraid that unsolicited flattery doesn't really do it for me and it still doesn't explain why

you're here. Why you burst into my hotel room unin-
vited and hid in my bathroom...*Leila.*'

For a moment there was silence.

Leila's heart pounded against her ribcage as she
heard the blatant challenge in his voice, which coun-
tered the silky way he emphasised her name. Her
mind was in a muddle and her senses felt raw and
exposed. She had taken a risk and she needed to follow it through, but it was proving more difficult than
she'd anticipated. Everything so far was going according to plan but suddenly she was filled with a powerful rush of nerves. She wondered how she could have
been so stupid. How she could have failed to take into
account Gabe Steel himself and the effect he would
have on her.

She looked into his grey eyes. Strange, quicksilver
eyes, which seemed to pierce her skin and see straight
through to the bones beneath. She tried to find the
right words to put her case to him, but everything
she'd been planning to say flew clean out of her mind.

She wasn't used to being alone with strange men
and she certainly wasn't used to being in a hotel room
with a foreigner. Especially one who looked like this.

He was gorgeous.

Unbelievably gorgeous.

She'd read up about him on the internet, of course.
She'd made it her business to do so once she'd discovered that her brother was going to employ him. She'd
found out all the external things about Gabe Steel. She
knew he owned Zeitgeist—one of the world's biggest
advertising agencies. That he'd been a millionaire by
the age of twenty-four and had made it into multi-
millions by the time he reached thirty. At thirty-five,

he remained unmarried—though not for the lack of women trying to get a wedding ring on their finger. Or at least, not according to reports from the rather more downmarket sources.

She'd seen images of him, too. Crystal-clear images, which she'd gazed at with something approaching wonder as they'd flashed up onto her computer screen. Because Gabe Steel seemed to have it all—certainly in the physical sense. His golden-dark hair gave him the appearance of an ancient god, and his muscular body would have rivalled that of any Olympian athlete.

She'd seen photos of him collecting awards, dressed in an immaculate tuxedo. There had been a snatched shot of him—paparazzi, she assumed—wearing faded jeans and an open shirt as he straddled a huge motorbike, minus a helmet. On one level she had known that he was the type of man who would take your breath away when you met him for real. And she hadn't been wrong.

She just hadn't expected him to be so...charismatic.

Leila was used to powerful men. She had grown up surrounded by them. All her life, she'd been bossed around and told to show respect towards them. Told that men knew best. She gave a wry smile because she had witnessed how cruel and cold they could be. She'd seen them treat women as if they didn't matter. As if their opinions were simply to be tolerated rather than taken seriously. Which was one of the reasons why, deep down, she didn't actually *like* the opposite sex.

Oh, she deferred to them, as she had been taught, because that was the hand which fate had dealt her.

To be born a princess into a fiercely male-dominated society didn't leave you with much choice other than to defer. There hadn't been a single major decision in her life which had been hers and hers alone. Her schooling had been decided without any consultation; her friends had been carefully picked. She had learnt to smile and accept—because she had also learnt that resistance was futile. People knew what was 'best' for her—and she had no alternative but to accept their judgement.

Materially, of course, she had been spoiled. When you were the only sister of one of the richest men in the world, that was inevitable. Diamonds and pearls, rubies and emeralds lay heaped in jewellery boxes in her bedroom at the palace. Her late mother's tiaras lay locked behind glass for Leila to wear whenever the mood took her.

But Leila knew that all the riches in the world couldn't make you feel good about yourself. Expensive jewels didn't compensate for the limitations of your lifestyle, nor protect you from a future you viewed with apprehension.

Within the confines of her palace home she usually dressed in traditional robes and veils, but today she was looking defiantly Western. She had never worn *quite* such figure-hugging jeans before and it was only by covering them up with her raincoat that she would have dared. She was aware of the way the thick seam of material rubbed between her legs. The way that the silky shirt felt oddly decadent as it brushed against her breasts. She felt *liberated* in these clothes, and while it was a good feeling, it was a little scary too—

especially as Gabe Steel was looking at her in a way which was curiously…*distracting*.

But her clothes were as irrelevant as his reaction to them. She had worn them in order to look modern and for no other reason. The most important thing to remember was that this man held the key to a different kind of future. And she was going to make him turn that key—whether he wanted to or not.

Fighting another wave of anxiety, she opened the briefcase she'd been holding and pulled out a clutch of carefully chosen contents.

'I'd like you to have a look at these,' she said.

He raised his eyebrows. 'What are they?'

She walked over towards a beautiful table and spread out the pictures on the gleaming inlaid surface. 'Have a look for yourself.'

He walked over to stand beside her, his dark shadow falling over her. She could detect the tang of lime and soap combined with the much more potent scent of masculinity. She remembered him wearing nothing but that tiny white towel and suddenly her mouth grew as dry as dust.

'Photographs,' he observed.

Leila licked her lips. 'That's right.'

She watched him study them and prayed he would like them because she had been taking photos for as long as she could remember. It had been her passion and escape—the one thing at which she'd shown real flair. But perhaps her position as princess meant that she was ideally placed to take photos, for her essentially lonely role meant that she was always on the outside looking in.

Ever since she'd been given her very first camera,

Leila had captured the images which surrounded her. The palace gardens and the beautiful horses which her brother kept in his stables had given way to candid shots of the servants and portraits of their children.

But most of the photos she'd brought to show Gabe Steel were of the desert. Stark images of a landscape she doubted he would have seen anywhere else and, since few people had been given access to the sacred and secret sites of Qurhah, they were also unique. And she suspected that a man like Gabe Steel would have seen enough in his privileged life to value something which was unique.

He was studying one in particular and she watched as his eyes narrowed in appreciation.

'Who took these?' he questioned, raising his head at last and capturing her in that cool grey gaze. 'You?'

She nodded. 'Yes.'

There was a pause. 'You're good,' he said slowly. 'Very good.'

His praise felt like a caress. Like the most wonderful compliment she had ever received. Leila glowed with a fierce kind of pride. 'Thank you.'

'Where is this place?'

'It's in the desert, close to the Sultan's summer palace. An area of outstanding natural beauty known as the Mekathasinian Sands,' she said, aware that his unsettling gaze was now drifting over her rather than the photo he was holding. He was close enough for her to be able to touch him, and she found herself wanting to do just that. She wanted to tangle her fingers in the thick, molten gold of his hair and then run them down over that hard, lean body. *And how crazy was that?*

With an effort, she tried to focus her attention on the photo and not on the symmetry of his chiselled features.

'I took this after one of the rare downpours of rain and subsequent flooding, which occur maybe once in twenty years, if you're lucky.' She smiled. 'They call it the desert miracle. Flower seeds lie dormant in the sands for decades and when the floods recede, they suddenly germinate—and flower. So that millions of blooms provide a carpet of colour which is truly magical—though it only lasts a couple of weeks.'

'It's an extraordinary picture. I've never seen anything like it.'

She could hear the sense of wonder in his voice and she felt another swell of pride. But suddenly, her work didn't seem as important as his unsettling proximity. She should have been daunted by that and she couldn't work out why she wasn't. She was alone in a hotel room with the playboy Gabe Steel and all she was aware of was a growing sense of excitement.

With an effort, she forced her attention back to the photo. 'If…if you look closely, you can see the palace in the distance.'

'Where?'

'Right over there.' The urge to touch him was overwhelming. It was the strongest impulse she'd ever felt, and suddenly Leila found herself unable to resist it. Leaning forward so that her arm brushed almost imperceptibly against his, she pointed out the glimmering golden palace. She felt his body stiffen as she made that barely there contact. She thought she could hear his breath catch in his throat. Was his heart hammering as hers was hammering? Was he too filled with an inexplicable sense of breathless wonder?

But he had stepped away from her, and his cool eyes were still curious. 'Why did you bring these photos here today, Leila? And more importantly, why were those men pursuing you?'

She hesitated. The truth was on her lips but she didn't dare say it. Because once he knew—he would change. People always did. He would stop treating her like an ordinary woman and start eyeing her warily—as if she were a strange creature he had never encountered before. And she was enjoying herself far too much to want him to do that.

So why not tell him part of the truth? The only part which was really important.

'I want to work for you,' she said boldly. 'I want to help you with your campaign.'

He raised his eyebrows in arrogant query. 'I don't recall advertising for any new staff,' he said drily.

'I realise that—but can't you see that it would make perfect sense?' Leaning forward, Leila injected real passion into her voice. 'I know Qurhah in a way you never can, because I grew up here and the desert is in my blood. I can point you in the direction of the best locations to show the world that our country is a particular kind of paradise. I've done plenty of research on what a campaign like yours would involve and I know there's room on this project for someone like me.'

She stared at him hopefully.

There was silence for a moment and then he gave a short laugh. 'You think I'd hire some unknown for a major and very lucrative campaign, just on the strength of a pretty face?'

Leila felt the sharp stab of injustice. 'But surely my "pretty face" has nothing to do with the quality of my work?'

'You don't think so?' He shot her a sardonic look. 'Well, I hate to disillusion you, sweetheart—but without the raven hair and killer figure I'd have kicked you out of here just as soon as those goons had gone.'

Leila tried to keep the sulk from her voice, because this was not what was supposed to happen. *She couldn't let it happen.* She narrowed her eyes in a way which would have made her servants grow wary if they had seen her. 'So you won't even consider me?'

'I won't consider anything until you satisfy my curiosity, and I am growing bored by your evasion. I'm still waiting for you to tell me who those men were.'

'My bodyguards,' she said reluctantly.

'Your *bodyguards*?'

She had surprised him now. She could see it in his face. She wondered how he would react if she told him the whole truth. That she had been born to be guarded. That people were always watching her. Stifling her. Making it impossible for her to breathe.

'I'm rich,' she said, by way of an explanation. 'In fact, I'm very rich.'

His grey eyes were speculative. 'So you don't *need* the work?'

'What kind of a question is that?' she questioned heatedly. 'I *want* to work! There's a difference, you know. I thought a man like you would appreciate that.'

Gabe acknowledged the reprimand in her voice. Yes, he knew there was a difference—it was just one which had never applied to him because he had always needed to work. There had been no wealth or legacy for him. No cushion waiting to bolster him if ever he fell. He had known only hunger and poverty. He had known what it was like to live beneath the radar and have your life subsumed by fear. He had needed to work for reasons of survival and for the peace of mind which always seemed determined to elude him. Even now.

'Oh, I appreciate it all right,' he agreed slowly.

'So you'll think about it? About hiring me?'

He looked down into her beautiful eyes and felt his heart twist with something like regret. He saw hope written in their azure depths—just as he saw all kinds of passionate possibilities written in her sensual lips. What would happen if he kissed this beautiful little rich girl who had marched into his hotel suite with such a sense of entitlement? Would she taste as good as she looked? He could feel the savage ache at his groin as he realised how badly he *wanted* to kiss her and for a moment temptation washed over him again.

But his innate cool professionalism reasserted itself and, regretfully, he shook his head. 'I'm sorry. I don't work that way. I run my organisation on rather more formal lines. If you really want to work for me, then I suggest you apply to my London office in the usual way. But I suspect that you've blown your chances anyway.' His eyes sent out a mocking challenge. 'You see, a long time ago I made a decision never to mix business with pleasure.'

She was staring at him, her nose wrinkling as if she was perplexed by his words. 'I don't understand.'

'Don't you?' He gave an unconvincing replica of a smile. 'Are you trying to tell me you haven't noticed the chemistry between us?'

'I—'

'Look, just take your photos and go,' he interrupted roughly. 'Before I do something I might live to regret.'

Leila heard his impatient words and some deep-rooted instinct urged her to heed them. To make her escape back to the palace while she still could and forget all about this crazy rebellion. Forget the fairy-tale ending of a legitimate job with the hotshot English tycoon. Forget the film-script scenario and get real. She needed to accept her life the way it was and accept that she couldn't just break out and change her entire existence.

But her thoughts were being confused by the powerful signals her body was sending out. She could feel the honeyed rush of heat between her thighs, where the thick seam of her jeans was rubbing against the most secret place of her body. She wanted to wrap her arms around her chest to try to quell the terrible aching in her breasts, yet she knew that would only draw attention to them.

Leila had read plenty of books and seen most of the current crop of films which had got past the palace censors. She might have been sheltered, but she wasn't stupid. This was sexual attraction she was experiencing for the first time and she knew it was *wrong*. Yet even as she silently urged herself to get out before she made even more of a fool of herself, those rebellious thoughts came back to plague her.

She thought about how her brother behaved. How

her own father had behaved. She'd heard the rumours about their sexual conquests often enough. She knew that men often acted on the kind of attraction she was experiencing right now, if the circumstances were right. People sometimes got intimate after nothing more than a short acquaintanceship, and nobody thought the worst of them for doing so. Because physical love wasn't a *crime*, was it?

Was it?

'What might you regret?' she asked, but she knew the answer to her question as soon as the words had left her lips. Because you wouldn't need to be experienced to realise why Gabe Steel's face had darkened like that. Or why he was staring at her with a hot, hard look which was making her feel weak.

'Does your mother know you're out?' he questioned roughly.

She shook her head. 'I don't have a mother. Or a father.' She kept her voice light, the way she'd learned to do. 'I'm just an orphan girl.'

His eyes narrowed. Darkened. He winced, as if she'd said something which had caused *him* pain.

'I'm sorry,' he said softly and reached out to brush the tip of his thumb over her lips. 'So sorry.'

The weirdest thing was that Leila wasn't sure if he was talking to her, or talking to himself. But suddenly she didn't care because it was happening—just like in all the films she'd seen. He was reaching out and pulling her into his arms and she could feel the heat of his body as he moulded it against her. He framed her face with the palms of his hands and now his mouth was coming down towards hers. He seemed to be moving in slow motion, and Leila felt weak with excitement as her lips parted eagerly to meet his.

Because for the first time in her life, a man was going to kiss her.

CHAPTER TWO

GABE FELT THE thunder of his heart as their mouths made that first contact. The warmth of her flesh collided with his and her skin smelt of flowers and spice. Desire flooded through him like fire but his hot lust was tempered by the cool voice of reason.

This was insane.

Insane.

He thought about the way she'd burst into his suite and the surly-faced bodyguards who might return at any time. It was obvious she shouldn't be here—and he was in danger of jeopardising a deal. A very important deal. He was here on business and due to dine at the Sultan's palace in a little under two hours. There wasn't time to make love to her properly—no matter how gloriously accessible she appeared to be.

So for God's sake, get rid of her!

But the moment he chose to push her away was the moment she chose to wind her arms around his neck and to move her body against his and to whisper something breathless in a language he didn't understand. The breath died in his throat as heat pooled in his groin and he was helpless to do anything other than deepen the kiss. He could feel the mound of her pubic bone pressing against his growing arousal—making his erection exquisitely hard and almost painful. Her tiny breasts were flattening themselves against his chest and, for the first time all day, his body felt warm instead of filled with the cold and aching memories of the past.

Tearing his mouth away, he stared down into her face, trying to ignore the provocative trembling of her lips. 'That was a mistake,' he said unsteadily. 'And I think you'd better get out of here before I make another one.'

'But what if I want you to?' she questioned breathlessly. 'What then?'

He felt another fierce stab of arousal as she looked at him. Her eyes were wide. Wide and bright. Shining as brightly as the aquamarine studs at her ears. He could feel his senses warring with his moral compass. *Send her away before it's too late.* But he couldn't stop looking at her or wanting her. Her lips were soft and gleaming. They looked as if they had been specially constructed to accommodate his erection and to suck him dry.

He thought about the dull pain nailed deep into his heart and how her soft body could alleviate it— even for an hour. Because sex could obliterate pain, couldn't it? He could feel his resolve slipping away from him, like sand through his fingers, and wondered if there was a man on earth who could have resisted what was being offered to him now.

'I'm giving you one last chance to get out of here,' he said unevenly. 'And I'd advise you to take it and go.'

'But I don't want to go anywhere,' she whispered. 'I want to stay right here.'

'Then I make no apologies for doing this,' he said. 'Which I have been wanting to do ever since you first walked in.'

He started to unbutton her shirt, exposing the silken flesh beneath, and another fierce jerk of desire shot through him. She was perfect, he thought. Just perfect. Her olive skin was dark against a brassiere so white that it looked as if she'd put it on new that morning. He drifted his fingertips over the gentle swell of her breast. 'So what have you got to say about that, *Leila*?'

Beneath the tantalising touch of his fingers, Leila grew weaker still. Where were the nerves she should be feeling? And why did it feel so natural? As if she had been waiting all her life for Gabe Steel to touch her like this?

'I think it's gorgeous,' she said, praying he wouldn't stop.

'I want to kiss your breasts,' he vowed unsteadily. 'Each beautiful breast which is peaking towards me, just waiting to be kissed.'

A pulse was hammering at his temple and Leila jerked with pleasure as he lowered his mouth to one tightening nipple. His dark blond head contrasted against the snowy silk of her bra, and she could feel the fabric growing moist as he sucked her. She squirmed in time to each provocative lick of his tongue, as helpless then as she could ever remember feeling. And suddenly she understood what all the fuss was about. Why sex was so powerful. Why people did such crazy things to get it.

'G-Gabe,' she gasped, the word stumbling over itself in disbelieving pleasure.

He lifted his head to stare at her, and suddenly his grey eyes were not so cold. They seemed bright with pewter fire.

'I think we're going to have to skip the next few stages,' he said. 'In fact, if I don't get you horizontal in the next couple of minutes, I think I'm going to go out of my mind.'

He caught hold of her fingers and led her straight into the bedroom she'd seen earlier—the bed still in rumpled disarray.

Now slightly disorientated, Leila looked around in faint bewilderment because she had never seen a room in such a state before. In her ordered and enclosed world, a servant would have attended to it while she'd been in the shower—making the bed all neat and pristine again and tidying away her discarded clothes.

She had never been lowered down onto untidy sheets which were still rich with the scent of the man who had slept in them. Nor towered over by someone whose mouth was tight as he continued to undress her. She stared up at him but he wasn't staring back. He was too busy removing her trainers and then unzipping her jeans as if he'd removed countless pairs of women's jeans in his life.

He probably had.

Of *course* he had.

Leila remembered what she'd read about him on the internet. Fragments of information about all the beautiful models and actresses he'd dated came drifting back. Women infinitely more experienced than she was.

She felt the cold shiver of insecurity reminding her to face facts and not be swept away by fantasy. She knew what men were like. How they were guided by the heat in their loins or the weight of their own ambition. She knew that they viewed women simply as possessions or as adornments—or as vessels to carry children.

She must not forget that.

This might feel as if she were living out a scene from a film, but it wasn't a film. This was real life and Gabe Steel wasn't suddenly going to turn into some fantasy hero and fall madly in love with her.

She didn't believe in that kind of love.

Her head fell back against the pillow as she felt the slide of his fingertips brushing over her thigh and suddenly it was difficult to think about anything, other than how good it felt.

He tugged the jeans down over her knees and she could hear the soft rustle as they fell to the floor.

'Nice knickers,' he murmured before deftly removing her bra and shirt.

Leila blushed at his words, telling herself this was normal. This was *natural*. 'Thanks,' she said, as if men complimented her on her choice of underwear every day of the week.

He tugged off his T-shirt and stood up to unbutton his jeans, and Leila was mesmerised as he peeled them off. Her heart began to pound with excitement as his body was revealed to her, for she had only ever seen a horse from the royal stables in such a state of arousal before.

Yet he seemed proud and unashamed of his nakedness as he walked across the room and retrieved something from his suitcase. Leila saw the glint of foil and the reality of what she was about to do suddenly hit her.

Because that was a condom; she was certain of it. She might never have encountered one before, but what else could it be?

She felt the icy clamp of sweat on her forehead as reality suddenly broke into her erotic thoughts. Did all women feel this sudden sense of panic the first time? The fear that she might disappoint him?

He was putting the item on the table beside the bed, and while she knew that she should be grateful to him for being pragmatic, it destroyed the mood a little. Why was real life so messy? she wondered bitterly. In films, you never saw any of *this*. Couples seemed to find themselves in bed together almost by magic and then the scene cut to them giggling as they ran down a street, usually in Paris. Not that she and Gabe Steel would be running anywhere here in Simdahab—at least not without the Sultan's guards giving chase. And if he didn't come back here and kiss her soon, she was going to get cold feet.

But almost as if he'd read her mind, he came back and lay down beside her. His body was warm, but his face was sombre as he traced a thoughtful line around her lips.

'Suddenly so serious,' he said, his grey eyes narrowing. 'As if you've started having regrets. Have you, Leila? Because we can stop this right now if that's what you want.'

Leila closed her eyes as she felt the brush of his finger over her lips. And wouldn't that be best? To put her clothes back on and get out of here as quickly as possible. She would feel embarrassed, and he might be angry with her for having led him on, but no real harm would have been done. She could slip away and act as if nothing had happened—because nothing had.

But then she thought about what awaited her back at the palace. She thought about all the inevitable restrictions and rules which had governed her life so far. All the things she wasn't allowed to do and never would be able to do *just because she was a woman and a princess*. She thought about the royal prince her brother would probably arrange for her to one day marry. The watchful eyes of both nations as they waited for her to produce an heir, before her husband thankfully sought refuge in the pleasures of his harem, just as her own father had done.

And suddenly she thought why *shouldn't* she experience this—as millions of other women had done? The way that men did *almost every day of their lives. Why shouldn't she have this one brief interlude of pleasure before she took up the duties which lay ahead of her?*

She wrapped her arms around his neck. 'Kiss me,' she whispered. 'Kiss me. Please.'

He smiled as his mouth came down to cover hers, and suddenly it *did* feel like a fairy tale. As if her senses had been fine-tuned. As if she were capable of anything. *Anything.*

'Oh,' she said, her eyes fluttering to a close as he drifted his mouth to her neck to kiss it over and over. 'Oh.'

Now his lips had found her breast and she could feel a thousand tiny sparks of pleasure as his tongue flicked against her puckered skin. She splayed her hands over his chest, where his heart pounded so strongly. She felt the coarse whorls of hair which grew there and she tugged at them—as playfully as a puppy with a new toy. His groan of delight filled her with confidence and she let her fingers drift downwards to explore the muscular flat of his belly and another helpless groan made her feel invincible. As if she could do anything or be anyone.

Anyone but herself.

He kissed her until she thought she would go out of her mind with longing. Until her heart was full of him. And suddenly, she wanted more. She could feel the restless movements of her body, orchestrated by a desire which seemed outside her understanding. Her fingers were kneading at his broad shoulders and she could hear him give a low laugh—as if her hunger pleased him. She could feel him tense as he began to nudge her legs apart with one insistent knee.

Her breath caught in her throat as he slid his hand between her thighs, and she cried out as he touched her where no man had ever touched her before.

'God, you're wet,' he groaned.

'Am I?' she questioned almost shyly.

'Mmm,' he affirmed as his finger began to strum against her, moving against her heated flesh in a light and silken rhythm.

Against his shoulder, Leila closed her eyes and felt as if she might melt beneath his touch. It felt gorgeous. He felt gorgeous. Gorgeous Gabe Steel who had stopped touching her and was now tearing at the little packet of foil he'd left beside the bed.

His face was formidable as he moved over her again and suddenly it was happening, almost without warning. He was lifting up her hips and making one deep, long thrust inside her, and she was crying out—only this time her cry sounded different, because the pain was very real. She felt him grow still and her heart plummeted as she saw the new expression on his face. The intense pleasure had changed into an expression of disbelief as he stared down at her.

'No,' he said, shaking his head. 'No.'

'What?' she gasped, because he was deep inside her and now that her body had adjusted to accommodate him, it felt amazing.

'You're a virgin?'

She sensed that he was about to pull out of her, but she had come this far and she couldn't bear him to stop. Some deep instinct was governing her now, and she prevented his withdrawal by the simply expedient of tightening her body around him. She saw his eyes grow at first angry and then smoky as tentatively she moved her hips upwards so that he was deeper still.

'So what if I am?' she whispered. 'Somebody's got to be the first and that somebody happens to be you. Please, Gabe. I want to experience pleasure the way that other women do. I want you to show me how. I know you can show me how.'

Gabe shook his head as he felt her slick heat yielding to his helpless thrust. The potent combination of her innocence and tightness and the erotic words she was whispering was making him harder than he could ever remember feeling before. But she was a virgin, he reminded himself. *Unbelievably, she was a virgin.* She had come to his room—this complete stranger—and given herself to him without any kind of ceremony. What kind of woman did that? He felt perplexed and resentful at having been lured into a situation which wasn't what it seemed.

So call a halt to it right now.

He swallowed. 'This is—'

'Heaven,' she said, her voice an irresistible murmur. 'You know it is. Don't stop, Gabe. Please don't stop.'

Her heartfelt plea was his final undoing. His anger evaporated and Gabe gave a groan of submission. Why fight it when she didn't want him to stop and... oh, God, neither did he? Pushing himself up on his elbows, he stared down at her beautiful face as he began to move inside her.

Her eyes were closed and he was glad about that. He didn't want to have to *look* at her; he just wanted to feel. He pushed deeper into her moist heat and groaned again, because she felt so good. She felt unbelievable. Was this why men spoke wonderingly about virgins, because they were so tight? Or because it gave a man a sense of power to know that he was the first?

But in the midst of all his macho triumph, he fought another wave of helplessness which was unfamiliar to him. Gone was the slick and seasoned Gabe who could last all night. He felt like a teenager who wanted instantly to explode inside her. But he mustn't. This had to be nothing less than amazing, because it was her first time. He *had* to take it slowly.

Yet it wasn't easy. He found himself stunned by the intense pleasure which was radiating through every pore of his body and not just because she was so tight. He realised how liberating it was not to have any emotional expectations hovering over him like a dark cloud. This really *was* sex without strings. Sex without the fear that she would fall in love with him and want more than he was ever prepared to give.

His thumb on her clitoris, he tilted her back against the pillows, listening to the rising volume of her cries. He watched as she began to move inexorably towards orgasm. Suddenly, she opened her eyes, and he met a clear flash of startled blue. As if she couldn't quite believe what was happening to her.

'Gabe?' she whispered, her accented voice unsteady.

'Relax.' He gave another deep thrust. 'Just. Let. Go.'

He saw her lips frame something which was destined never to be said as her eyelashes flew down to shutter out the blue. And then her body started to quiver helplessly around him and her back began to arch. He heard the words she said as she convulsed around him, although she spoke them in a language he didn't understand. He kissed away the muffled little cries which followed and tried to ignore her fingernails, which were now digging painfully into his back. He waited until her body was almost still before he let go himself, spilling out his seed in great wrenching bursts he never wanted to end.

For a moment he felt so dazed that it was almost as if he'd been drugged. Today, of all days—his body was warm and pulsing with life, instead of feeling empty and cold or deliberately anaesthetised. From between slitted eyes, he surveyed her. Her glossy black hair was tumbling down over her breasts and her perfect olive skin was flushed.

He lifted his hand to her cheek and felt her shiver beneath that light touch. 'Who are you?' he questioned, but she leaned over him and kissed his lips into silence.

'Shh,' she said, and her voice was very gentle. 'You look weary. Go to sleep, Gabe. Just go to sleep.'

CHAPTER THREE

'HAVE YOU BEEN listening to a word I've been saying, Leila?'

Leila gave a start as her brother's impatient question cut through the confusion of her thoughts. In the air-conditioned cool of the palace, she wondered if the hectic colour had faded from her cheeks and for once she gave thanks to the veil which concealed them from the Sultan. But there were other signs, too. She knew that. The mirror had told her so when she'd looked in it a short while ago.

Had the telltale glitter disappeared from her eyes? She prayed it had. Because if her clever and dictatorial brother Murat ever guessed how she had spent that particular afternoon...

If he had any idea that she had given her virginity to a man who had been a stranger to her.

She shivered.

He would kill her.

'Of course I was listening,' she defended.

His black eyes narrowed. 'So I was saying...what?'

Leila swallowed as she searched around in the fog of her memory for something to remind her. 'Something about the banquet you're holding tonight.'

'Very good, Leila.' He nodded. 'It seems you were paying attention, after all. A banquet in honour of my English guest, Gabe Steel.'

The sudden tremble of her knees at the mention of his name made Leila glad that she was sitting down. 'Gabe Steel?' she echoed and his name tasted nearly as sweet on her lips as his kisses had done.

Murat gave an impatient click of his tongue. 'He is coming here tonight. You *knew* that, Leila.'

Leila forced a smile, acknowledging the power of the human mind to deny something which made you feel uncomfortable. It was the same as going for a ride in the desert—you knew that in the sand lurked snakes and scorpions, but if you thought about them for too long you'd never get on a horse again.

Of course she had known that Gabe was coming here tonight but—as with all the Sultan's formal banquets—she hadn't been invited. If she had, then there would have been no need to have gone to the advertising executive's room in secret to make her doomed job application. And then to have acted like some kind of…

Briefly, she closed her eyes. She mustn't think about him. She mustn't.

Yet try as she might, it was impossible to stem the flashbacks which plagued her, as if someone were playing a forbidden and erotic movie inside her head on an endless loop. She couldn't seem to stop remembering the way he'd made love to her and the way he had made her feel.

She knew that what she had done today had been wrong. It had flown in the face of everything she had been brought up to believe in. In Qurhah, women who were 'good' saved themselves until marriage. Especially royal princesses. There was simply no other option and up until today she had never questioned it. Yet she had seized the opportunity to let the powerful tycoon take her to his bed without a second thought. She had wanted him with a hunger which had taken her by surprise, and he had wanted her just as much, it seemed. For the first time in her life, she had behaved in a way which was truly liberated.

She remembered the gleam of his dark golden hair against the white of the pillow after he'd made that strange low cry and shuddered deep inside her. The way he had fallen asleep almost immediately—a sleep so deep that for a moment she'd had to check he was still breathing. He hadn't even stirred when she'd slipped from the bed—her body still warm and aching and her skin suffused with a soft, warm glow.

Silently, she had crept around the hotel suite—gathering up her discarded clothes, which she'd put on in the bathroom with trembling fingers, terrified that he would hear. And she hadn't wanted him to hear. She had known that her only option was to slip away before he awoke because she couldn't face saying goodbye, Not when she was feeling in such a volatile emotional state and she wanted nothing more than to snuggle into his warm embrace and kiss those sensual lips of his again.

Because that was simply not on the cards. There was no future for them. She knew that. Not now and not ever—and she sensed that in her vulnerable post-orgasm state she might have been tempted to overlook that simple fact.

She sucked in a deep breath, telling herself that

what was done was done and she wasn't going to feel ashamed about something she had enjoyed so much. Not when for the first time in her life she had behaved like a free-thinking woman instead of a puppet whose strings were constantly being pulled by her powerful brother, the Sultan.

But she could also see now that her thinking had been skewed. She had been foolishly naive to approach the Englishman in the first place. Had she really imagined that Gabe Steel—no matter how powerful he was in his own country—could persuade her brother to let her work with him? Did she really think she could go from pampered princess to Westerner's aide in one easy transition?

She could feel Murat's eyes on her and knew he was waiting for some kind of response. He might be her brother, but he was first and foremost the Sultan—and, as such, the world always revolved around Murat.

'There is no need for me to express my hope that your banquet will be successful, Murat,' she said formally. 'For that is a given.'

There was a pause as he inclined his head, silently acknowledging her praise.

'I thought you might wish to attend,' he said.

For the second time, Leila was glad she was sitting down. She narrowed her eyes, thinking she must have misheard him. 'The banquet?'

The Sultan shrugged his shoulders. 'Why not?'

'Why not?' She laughed. 'Is that a serious question? Because it's "business" and these affairs are traditionally men only.'

Murat gave a little shake of his shoulders and Leila thought he seemed a little *unsettled* tonight. Which wasn't like her brother at all. Maybe the cancellation of his arranged marriage had affected him more than it had appeared to do at the time.

'Then perhaps it is time that Qurhah embraced the untraditional for a change,' he said.

Leila stared at him in growing disbelief. 'What on earth has brought all this on?'

Murat glowered. 'Does there have to be a reason for everything? You have harangued me for many years for a more inclusive role in state affairs, Leila—'

'And you always ignore everything I say!'

'And now that I am actually proposing a break in tradition,' he continued implacably, 'I am being subjected to some sort of inquisition!'

Leila didn't answer because her heart had grown disconcertingly light. She tried to ignore the flutter in her stomach and the rush of blood to her cheeks, but she couldn't ignore the glorious words which were circling round and round in her mind. She had been invited to the banquet! She was going to see Gabe again!

Her heart pounded. How would it feel to face him again at a formal palace dinner? And how would he react to seeing her in the last place he would ever expect to see her?

She felt the sudden rush of nerves and sternly she told herself not to get carried away. It didn't matter how he reacted because that was irrelevant. Yes, he had been the kind of lover that every woman dreamt of, but Gabe was just a man. And she knew about men. She knew about the pain and heartbreak they caused women. The muffled sound of her mother's tears had characterised her childhood and she reminded herself not to weave any foolish dreams about Gabe Steel.

'You are very quiet, Leila,' observed the Sultan softly. 'I had imagined you would be delighted to meet my Western guest.'

Leila gave a cautious smile. 'Forgive me for my somewhat muted response,' she said. 'For I was a little taken off-guard by your unexpected generosity. Naturally, I shall be delighted to meet Mr Steel.'

'Good. And you will wear the veil, of course. I like the thought of our Western visitor observing the quiet decorum of the traditional Qurhahian woman.' Murat frowned. 'Though I hope you're not coming down with a fever, Leila—for your complexion has suddenly grown very flushed.'

Gabe barely registered the gleaming golden gates which had opened to allow his bulletproof car through. Just as he had failed to register the colourful and bustling streets of Simdahab on his way to the palace. The journey through the city had been slower than he had anticipated—mainly, he suspected, because the car was so heavily armoured. He guessed that was one of the drawbacks to being a fabulously powerful sultan—that the risk of assassination was never far from the surface.

Yet instead of focusing on the task ahead or reflecting on the cultural differences between the two countries, as he usually would have done, he had spent the entire journey thinking about the woman it was probably safer to forget.

Leila.

When he'd woken from a deep sleep in that sex-rumpled bed, he had known a moment of complete and utter peace—before disjointed memories had come flooding back. For a moment he'd thought that he must have dreamt the whole bizarre incident. And then he had seen the faint red spots of blood on the sheet—not knowing if it had sprung from her broken hymen or when her fingernails had clawed deep into the flesh of his shoulders at the moment of orgasm.

He stared out of the car window at the vast splendour of the palace gardens, but this faint feeling of disorientation would not leave him.

He had always been successful with women—and not just because of his hard body and what the press had once described as his 'fallen angel' looks. He had quickly learnt how best to handle the opposite sex, because he could see that it was in his best interests to do so. To take what he wanted without giving any false hope. He'd learnt that guaranteeing pleasure was the most effective way of having someone overlook your shortcomings—the main one being his aversion to emotion. He knew that he couldn't give love—but he could certainly give great orgasms.

He'd seen it all and done it all—or so he'd thought—though he'd avoided any situation involving cameras or threesomes. But he had never had a beautiful, virginal stranger turning up at his hotel room and allowing him to seduce her within minutes of meeting.

He felt his heart miss a beat as he recalled the way she had made him feel. That initial hard thrust against her tight hymen. Who *was* she? And why had she chosen to give her innocence to a man she didn't know?

He thought about the photographs she'd shown him. Nobody could deny that she was talented. Did she think that her sexual generosity would guarantee her the offer of a job? Yet if that was the case, then surely she would have left him her card—or some number scribbled down on a sheet of hotel notepaper, so that he could contact her again. But she hadn't. There had been nothing to mark the fact that she'd been there. Only her very feminine fragrance lingering with the unmistakeable scent of sex when he'd woken to find an empty space beside him and silence in the adjoining suite of rooms.

Gabe shook his head as the limousine drew to a halt and a robed servant opened the door for him. He must put her out of his mind and concentrate on the evening ahead. It didn't matter who his mystery virgin was. It had happened and it was over. He could shut the door on it, just as he did with every other aspect of his past. He was here at the palace to meet formally with the Sultan and none of the other stuff mattered.

Buttoning up the jacket of his suit, he stepped out onto the honey-coloured gravel of the forecourt and in the distance he could see a long line of similar limousines already parked. The turreted palace gleamed red-gold in the light of the setting sun, like something out of an upmarket Disney film. Gabe wondered how long it had taken to build this impressive citadel—an unmistakeable symbol of beauty and power, set in an oasis of formal and surprisingly green gardens.

The evening air was thick with the scent of roses and soft with the sound of running water from the stream which traversed the palace grounds. In the distance, he could see soaring mountain peaks topped with snow and, closer, the circular and steady flight of what looked like a bird of prey.

That was what he should be thinking about, he reminded himself grimly. Not a woman who had made him feel slightly...

He frowned.

Used?

Had she?

'Gabe! Here you are at last. May I welcome you to my home?'

An accented voice broke into his thoughts. Gabe turned to find the Sultan standing on the steps to greet him. A tall and imposing figure, he was framed by the dramatic arches of the palace entrance behind him. His robes and headdress were pure white and the starkness of his appearance was broken only by the luminosity of his olive skin. For a moment, a distant memory floated across Gabe's mind before it disappeared again, like a butterfly on a summer's day.

Gabe smiled. 'Your Most Imperial Highness,' he said. 'I am most honoured to be invited to your palace.'

'The honour is all mine,' said the Sultan, stepping forward to shake him warmly by the hand. 'How was London when you left?'

'Rainy,' said Gabe.

'Of course it was.' The two men exchanged a wry look.

Gabe had first met the Sultan at the marriage of one of his own employees. At the time, Sara Williams had been working as a 'creative' at his advertising agency before she'd ruffled a few feathers by bringing her rather complicated love-life into the office.

During that rather surreal wedding day in the nearby country of Dhi'ban, the Sultan had told Gabe that he knew of his formidable reputation and asked if he would help bring Qurhah into the twenty-first century by helping change its image. Initially, Gabe had been reluctant to accept such a potentially tricky commission, but it had provided a challenge, in a life where fresh challenges were rare.

And he had timed it to coincide with an anniversary which always filled him with guilt and regret.

'You are comfortable at your hotel?' asked the Sultan.

For a moment, Gabe felt erotic recall trickle down his spine. 'It's perfect,' he said. 'One of the most beautiful buildings I've ever stayed in.'

'Thank you. But you will find our royal palace more beautiful still.' The Sultan made a sweeping gesture with his hand. 'Now come inside and let me show you a little Qurhahian hospitality.'

Gabe followed the monarch through the long corridors of the palace, made cool by the soft breeze which floated in from the central courtyard. Past bowing ranks of servants, they walked—overlooked by portraits of hawk-faced kings from ages gone by, all of whom bore a striking resemblance to his host.

It was more than a little dazzling but the room which they entered defied all expectation. Tall and as impressive as a cathedral, the high-ceilinged chamber was vaulted with the soft gleam of gold and the glitter of precious gems. People stood chatting and sipping their drinks, but the moment the Sultan entered everyone grew silent and bowed their heads in homage.

What must it be like to have that kind of power over people? wondered Gabe as he was introduced first to the Sultan's emissary and then to a whole stream of officials—all of them men. Some of them—mainly the older generation—were clearly suspicious of a foreigner who had been brought in to tamper with the image of a country which had always fiercely prided itself on its national identity. But Gabe knew that change inevitably brought with it pain, and so he listened patiently to some of the reservations which were being voiced before the bell rang for dinner.

He accompanied Sultan into a vast dining room, where lavishly laid tables were decorated with fragrant roses coloured deep crimson. Inexplicably, he found his eyes flickering towards their dark petals and wondering why the sight of them unsettled him so. Like the blood on his sheets, he thought suddenly—and a whisper of apprehension iced his skin.

'I have seated you next to the Ambassador of Maraban, who is one of the most influential men in the region,' said the Sultan. 'With my sister on the other side. Her English is excellent and she is eager to meet with you, for she meets few Westerners. Ah, here she comes now. Leila!'

But Gabe didn't need to hear his host say her name to know the woman's identity. He knew that from the moment she entered the banqueting hall. Even though her body was swathed in flowing silk and even though a matching veil of palest silver was covering half her face, there could be no mistaking her. No amount of camouflage could disguise that sexy sway of her body—or maybe it was because in some primeval and physical way, he still felt connected to her.

He could still smell her on his skin.

He could still taste her in his mouth.

He could still remember the exact moment when

he had broken through her tightness and claimed her for his own.

Why the hell had she kept her identity hidden from him?

The Sultan was saying something, and Gabe had to force himself to listen and to pray that the sudden clamour of his senses would settle.

'Leila.' The hawk-faced leader smiled. 'This is Gabe Steel—the advertising genius from London of whom you have heard me speak. Gabe, I'd like you to meet Princess Leila Scheherazade of Qurhah—my only sister.'

For a moment Gabe was so angry he could barely get a word out in response, but he quickly asserted the self-possession which was second nature to him. He had worked all his life in an industry which traded on illusion and knew only too well how to wear whichever mask the occasion demanded. And so he produced the slightly deferential smile he knew was expected of him on meeting the royal princess. He even inclined his head towards her, before catching a peep of a crystal-encrusted sandal which was poking out from beneath the folds of her gown. And the sight of those beautiful toes sent a surge of anger and lust shooting through him.

'I am honoured to meet you, Your Royal Highness,' he said, but as he straightened up he saw the sudden colour which flushed over the upper part of her face. He saw the brief flicker of distress which flared in the depths of her blue eyes. And that distress pleased him. His mouth hardened. It pleased him very much.

'The pleasure is also mine, Mr Steel,' she said softly.

'Leila, please show our guest to his place.' The

Sultan clapped his hands loudly, and once again the room grew silent. 'And let us all be seated.'

Silently, Gabe followed Leila across the dining room and took his place beside her. In the murmured moments as two hundred guests sat down, he seized the opportunity to move his head close to hers. 'So. Are you going to give me some kind of explanation?'

'Not now,' she said calmly.

'I want some sort of explanation, Your Royal *Highness*.'

'Not now,' she repeated, and then she lifted her fingers and began to remove her veil.

And despite the anger still simmering away inside him, Gabe held his breath as her features were slowly revealed to him. Because in a world where nudity was as ubiquitous as the cell phone, this was the most erotic striptease he had ever witnessed.

First he saw the curve of her chin and, above that, those sensual lips, which looked so startlingly pink against her luminous skin. He remembered how those lips had felt beneath the hard crush of his own and he felt himself harden instantly. He tried to tell himself that her nose was too strong and aquiline for conventional beauty and that there were women far more lovely than her. But he was lying—because in that moment she looked like the most exquisite creature he had ever seen.

And she had deceived him. She had lied to him as women always lied.

Taking a long draught of wine in an effort to steady his nerves, somehow he hung on to his temper for as long as it took to charm the ambassador during the first course, which he had no desire to eat.

He wondered if it was rude to completely ignore Leila, but he didn't care—because he still didn't trust himself to speak to her again. It wouldn't look good if he exploded with anger at the exalted banqueting table of the Sultan, would it? Yet he found his gaze drawn inexorably to the way her fingers toyed with the heavy golden cutlery as she pushed food around her plate.

The ambassador had turned away to talk to the person on his left and Gabe took the opportunity to lean towards her, his voice shaking with suppressed rage. 'So is there some kind of power game going on that I should know about, Leila?' he said. 'Some political intrigue which will slowly be revealed to me as the evening progresses?'

Her heavy golden fork clattered to her plate and he saw the apprehension on her face as she turned to face him.

'There's no intrigue,' she answered, her voice as low as his.

'No? Then why all the mystery? Why not just tell your brother that we've already met. Unless he doesn't know, of course.'

'I—'

'Maybe he has no idea that his sister came to my hotel today,' he continued remorselessly. 'And let me—'

'Please.' Her interruption sounded anguished. 'We can't talk here.'

'Then where do you suggest?' he questioned. 'Same time, same place tomorrow? Maybe you'd already planned to return for a repeat performance, wearing a different kind of disguise. Maybe the mas-

querade aspect turns you on. I don't know.' His eyes
bored into her. 'Had you?'

'Mr Steel—'

'It's Gabe,' he said with icy pleasantry. 'You remember how to say my name, don't you, Leila?'

Briefly, Leila closed her eyes. She certainly did.
And she hadn't just *said* it, had she? She'd gasped it
as he had entered her. She had whispered it as he'd
moved deep inside her. She had shuddered it out in a
long, keening moan as her orgasm had taken hold of
her and almost torn her apart with pleasure.

And now all those amazing memories were being
swept away by the angry wash from his eyes.

She wished she could spirit herself away. That she
could excuse herself by saying she felt sick—which
was actually true, because right at that moment she
did feel sick.

But Murat would never forgive her if she interrupted the banquet—why, it might even alert his suspicions if he suspected that she found the Englishman's
presence uncomfortable. He might begin to ask himself why. And surely the man beside her—*the man
who had made such incredible love to her*—couldn't
keep up this simmering hostility for the entire meal?

'Look, I can understand why you're angry,' she
said, trying to keep her tone conciliatory.

'Can you?' His pewter eyes glittered out a hostile
light. 'And why might that be? Because you failed to
reveal your true identity to me?'

'I wasn't—'

'Or because it's only just occurred to you that you
might have compromised my working relationship
with your brother?' His voice was soft but his words

were deadly. 'Because no man likes to discover that his sister has behaved like a whore.'

He leaned back in his chair to study her, as if they were having a perfectly amicable discussion, and Leila thought how looks could deceive. The casual observer would never have noticed that the polite smile on his lips was completely at odds with the angry glitter in his grey eyes.

'I was behaving as other women sometimes behave,' she protested. 'Spontaneously.'

'But most women aren't being pursued by bodyguards at the time,' he continued. His voice lowered, and she could hear the angry edge to his words. 'What would have happened if they had burst in and found us in bed together?'

Leila tried desperately to block the image from her mind. 'I don't know.'

'Oh, I think you've got a pretty good idea. What would have happened, Leila?'

She swallowed, knowing that he was far too intelligent to be fobbed off with a vague answer. 'You would have been arrested,' she admitted reluctantly.

'I would have been arrested,' he repeated grimly and nodded his head. 'Destroying my reputation and losing my freedom in the process. Maybe even my head?'

'We are not that barbaric!' she protested, but her words did not carry the ring of conviction.

'It's funny really,' he continued, 'because for the first time in my life I'm feeling like some kind of stud. Wham and bam—but not much in the way of thank you, ma'am.'

'No!' she said. 'It wasn't like that.'

'Really? Then what was it? Love at first sight?'

Leila picked up her goblet of black cherry juice and drank a mouthful, more as a stalling mechanism than because she was thirsty. His words were making her realise just how impulsive she had been and how disastrous it would have been if they'd been caught. But they *hadn't* been caught, had they? Maybe luck—or fate—had been on their side.

And the truth of it was that her heart had leapt with a delicious kind of joy when she'd seen him again tonight, in his charcoal suit and a silver tie the colour of a river fish. She had stared at the richness of his hair and longed to run her fingers through it. Her eyes had drifted hungrily over his hard features and, despite everything she'd vowed not to do, she had wanted to kiss him. She had started concocting unrealistic little fantasies about him, and that was crazy. Just because he had proved to be an exquisite lover, didn't mean that she should fall into that age-old female trap of imagining that he had a heart.

Because no man had a heart, she reminded herself bitterly.

'Love?' She met the challenge in his eyes. 'Why, do you always have to be in love before you can have sex?'

'Me? No. Most emphatically I do not. But women often do, especially when it's their first time. But then I guess most women aren't just spoiled little princesses who see what they want and go out and take it—and to hell with the consequences.'

Leila didn't react to the *spoiled-little-princess* insult. She knew people thought it, though no one had ever actually come out and said it to her face before.

She knew what people thought about families like hers and how they automatically slotted her into a gilded box marked 'pampered'. But what they saw wasn't always the true picture. Unimaginable wealth didn't protect you from the normal everyday stuff. Glittering palace walls didn't work some kind of magic on the people who lived within them. Prick her skin and she would bleed, just like the next woman.

'It was an unconventional introduction, I admit,' she said. 'To bring my work to your hotel room unannounced like that and ask you for a job.'

'Please don't be disingenuous, Leila. That's not what I'm talking about and you know it.' He sounded impatient now. 'Which guide to interview technique did you study before you started removing your clothes and climbing all over me? *The 1960s Guide to Sexual Behaviour*? Or *A Hundred Ways To Make The Casting Couch Work For You*?'

'You didn't seem so averse to the idea at the time!'

'Funny that,' he mused. 'A beautiful woman comes up to my suite, turns her big blue eyes on me and starts coming on to me. She brushes my arm so lightly that I wonder if I'd imagined it, though my senses tell me I hadn't. Then she pirouettes around so that there can be no mistaking the tight cut of her jeans or the cling of her blouse as she shows off her amazing body. She gazes into my eyes as if I am the answer to all her prayers.' *And for one brief moment hadn't he felt as if he could be?*

There was a pause as Leila forced herself to scoop some jewel-coloured rice onto her fork—terrified that someone might notice that she hadn't eaten a thing and start asking themselves why. Had she done everything which Gabe had accused her of? Had she behaved like some kind of *siren*? She lifted her head to look at him. 'You could have stopped me,' she said.

Gabe stilled as he met the challenge sparking from her blue eyes. Because hadn't he been thinking the same thing ever since it had happened? He could have stopped her. He *should* have stopped her. He should have waited until her bodyguards had gone and then told her to get out of his room as quickly as possible. He could have dampened down his desire, using the formidable self-control which had carried him through situations far more taxing than one of sexual frustration. He could have told her that he didn't have a type, but that if he did—she wouldn't be it.

He didn't like women who were *obvious*. Who had persistent exes or *brothers who were sultans*. He had an antenna for women who were trouble and it had never failed him before. He resisted the tricky ones. The neurotic and needy ones.

But something had gone wrong this time.

Because he hadn't resisted Leila, had he? He had broken his own rules and taken her to bed without knowing a single damned thing about her. And he still couldn't work out why. He shook his head slightly. It had been something indefinable. Something in those wide blue eyes which had drawn him in. He had felt like a man whose throat was parched. Who had been shown a pool of water and invited to drink from it. He had felt almost…

His eyes narrowed.

Almost *helpless*.

And that was never going to happen.

Not twice in a lifetime.

'I could have stopped you,' he agreed slowly.

'So why didn't you?'

He didn't answer straight away because it was important to get this right. He wanted to send out a message to her. A very clear message she could not fail to understand. That it had meant nothing to him. That it would be a mistake to fall for him. That he caused women pain. Deep pain.

'Sometimes sex is like an itch,' he said deliberately. 'And you just can't help yourself from scratching it.'

Her face didn't register any of the kind of emotions he might have expected. No indignation or hurt. He suspected that hers was a world where feelings as well as faces were hidden. But he saw her eyes harden, very briefly. As if he had simply confirmed something she had already known.

'I'm sure that the romantic poets need have nothing to fear from your observations,' she said sarcastically.

He picked up his goblet of wine, twirling the long golden stem between his fingers. 'Just so long as we understand each other.'

She leaned forward, and he caught a drift of some faint scent. It made him think of meadow flowers being crushed underfoot. He found it...*distracting*.

'Oh, I get the message loud and clear,' she said. 'So forgive me if I ignore you as much as possible for the rest of the meal. I think we've said everything there is to say to each other, don't you?'

CHAPTER FOUR

LEILA GRIPPED THE side of the washbasin as terror sliced through her like the cold blade of a sword. She wanted to scream. Or to throw back her head and howl like an animal. But she didn't dare. Because her fear of discovery was almost as great as the dark suspicion which had been growing inside her for days.

She stayed perfectly still and listened, her heart thudding painfully in her chest. Had anyone heard her? Had one of the many unseen servants been close enough to the bathroom to catch the sound of her shuddered retching?

She closed her eyes.

Please no.

But when she opened them again, she knew that she could no longer keep pretending. She couldn't keep hoping and praying that this wasn't happening, because it was.

It had started with a missed period. One day late. Two days late—then a full week. Her nerves had been shot. Her heart seemed to have been permanently racing with horror and fear. She was *never* late—her monthly cycle was as reliable as the morning sunrise. And the awful thing was that she'd had to *pretend* that it had arrived. She'd forced herself to wince and to clutch at the lower part of her stomach as if in discomfort, desperate not to alert the suspicions of her female servants. Because in that enclosed, watched world of the palace, nothing went unnoticed—not even the princess's most intimate secrets.

She had told herself that it was just a glitch. That it must be her body behaving in an unusual way because it had been introduced to sex. Then she had tried not thinking about it at all. When that hadn't worked, she'd made silent pleas to Mother Nature, promising that she would be good for the rest of her life, if only she wasn't carrying Gabe Steel's baby.

But her pleas went unanswered. The horror was real. The bare and simple fact wasn't going away, simply because she wanted it to.

She was pregnant.

Her one brief experiment with sex—her one futile attempt to behave with the freedom of a man—had left her with a consequence which was never going to leave her. Pregnant by a man who never wanted to see her again.

She was ruined.

With trembling fingers, she tidied her mussed hair, knowing she couldn't let her standards slip. She had to maintain the regal facade expected of her, because if anyone ever *guessed*...

She thought about the meagre options which lay open to her and each of them filled her with foreboding. She thought what would happen if her brother found out, and a shudder ran down her spine. She gripped the washbasin, and the cold porcelain felt like ice beneath her clammy fingers. Murat must not find out—at least, not yet.

She was going to have to tell Gabe.

But Gabe had gone back to England and there were no plans for her to see him again. He had spent a further fortnight working here in Qurhah without their paths ever crossing. Why would they? He had made it clear that he wanted to forget what had happened and she had convinced herself she felt the same way. She'd found herself reflecting how strange it was that two people who'd been so intimate could afterwards act like strangers.

Even the farewell dinner given in honour of the English tycoon had yielded no moments of closeness. She and Gabe had barely exchanged any words at all, bar a few stilted ones of greeting. During the meal she'd read nothing but cool contempt in his pewter eyes. And that had hurt. She had experienced for the first time the pain of rejection, made worse by the dull ache of longing.

Her mind working overtime, Leila shut the bathroom door behind her and walked slowly back to her private living quarters. Gabe Steel might not be her first port of call in normal circumstances, but right now he was the only person she could turn to.

She had to tell him.

But how?

She looked out over the palace rose gardens where the bright orange bloom which had been named after her in the days following her birth was now in glorious display.

If she phoned him, who wasn't to say that some interfering palace busybody might not be listening in to her call? And phoning him would still leave her here, pregnant and alone and vulnerable to the Sultan's rage if he found out.

But if she left it much longer it was inevitable he would find out anyway.

A sudden knock at the door disturbed her, and her troubled thoughts became magnified when one of her servants informed her that the Sultan wished to see her with immediate effect.

Leila's mouth was dry with fear as she walked silently along the marble corridors towards Murat's own magnificent section of the royal palace. Had he guessed? Was he summoning her to tell her that she had brought shame on the royal house, and that she was to be banished to some isolated region of their vast country to bring up her illegitimate child in solitude?

But when she was ushered into his private sitting room, Murat's demeanour was unusually solicitous, his black eyes narrowed with something almost approaching *concern*.

He began by asking whether she was well.

'Yes, I am very well,' she lied, praying that her horror at this particular question would not show on her face. 'Why…why do you ask?'

Murat shrugged. 'Just that you seem to have been almost invisible lately. You don't seem to have been yourself at all. Is something wrong, Leila?'

He'd *noticed*!

Despite her wild flare of fear, Leila knew that she must not react. She must not give her clever brother any inkling that she was concealing a desperate secret. With a resourcefulness she wasn't aware she possessed—though maybe desperation was in itself an inspiration—Leila shrugged. 'I have been feeling a little discontented of late.'

His eyes narrowed. 'In what way?'

She licked her lips. 'I feel as if I have seen nothing of the world, or of life itself. All I know is Qurhah.'

'That is because you are a princess of Qurhah,' Murat growled. 'And your place is here.'

'I know that,' said Leila, thinking that he made her sound like an ancient piece of furniture which had never been moved from its allocated place on the rug. 'But you travel. You get to visit other countries. And I...I have seen nothing of the world, other than the surrounding lands of the desert region.'

The Sultan's black eyes narrowed. 'And?'

She forced herself to say the words, to make him think that she had accepted the future which had been planned for her. A future which could now never happen, because what prospective royal husband would wish to take a bride who carried another man's child?

'I know that my place is here, Murat,' she said quietly. 'But before I immerse myself in the life which has been mapped out for me—could I not have an overseas trip?'

Beneath his silken headdress, Murat's dark brows knitted together. 'What kind of trip?' he echoed.

Leila could hardly believe she'd got this far and knew she mustn't blow it now. She thought about the tiny, forbidden life growing inside her and she drew in a deep breath. 'You know that Princess Sara has a place in London?'

'So I gather,' said Murat carelessly.

Leila watched her brother's reaction closely, but if

he was hurt to hear the name of the woman he'd once been betrothed to, he didn't show it.

'She often writes to me and tells me all about the fabulous shopping in the city,' Leila continued. 'Many times she has asked me to visit her there. Couldn't I do that, Murat—just for a few days? You know how much I love shopping!'

There was silence for a moment. Had she made her request sound suitably fluffy? If she'd told her brother that she wanted to go and see a photographic exhibition which was being launched, he would never have approved. He was one of those men who believed that shopping kept women subdued. Lavish them with enough *stuff* and it kept them satisfied.

'I suppose that a few days could be arranged,' he said eventually.

Leila gave a little squeal of joy—showing her brother the gratitude she knew would be expected of her—but it was with a heavy heart that she packed for her forthcoming trip. She thought about the terrifying secret she carried. About how humiliating it was to have to seek out a man who did not want her, to tell him something he would be appalled to hear.

Arrangements were made between the palace and Princess Sara, who Leila had known since she'd been a child. Sara had once been promised to Murat himself but was now married to Suleiman, and they had homes all around the world.

With a retinue of bodyguards and servants, Leila flew by private jet to England where they took over the entire top floor of the Granchester Hotel in central London. She was one step closer to Gabe. One step closer to sharing her news—and didn't they say that a problem shared was a problem halved?

But then she remembered his cold face as she'd sat beside him at the banquet. She forced herself to recall the fact that he had never wanted to see her again. There was to be no fairy-tale ending with this man, she reminded herself sombrely. She looked out of the penthouse windows of her hotel suite, across a beautiful park alive with flowers—and a terrible feeling of isolation came over her.

She could see couples openly walking together—their arms looped around each other as they kissed. A young child chased a dog and, behind him, a woman wheeled a pram. Everyone seemed part of the world which lay before her eyes—all except her. And Leila couldn't remember ever feeling quite so alone as she did right then.

Knowing she couldn't keep putting off the dreaded moment much longer, she picked up the hotel phone and dialled Gabe's office, her heart pounding with apprehension. She had to go through two different people before his voice came on the line, and when it did—he sounded distant.

Wary.

Terror gripped her as she realised she was about to drop a live grenade into his perfect life.

'Leila?'

'Yes, it's me. How…how are you, Gabe?'

'I am well.' There was a pause. 'This is a surprise.'

'I imagine it is.' She drew in a deep breath. 'Look, I need to see you.'

'I thought we'd agreed that wasn't such a good idea.

And anyway, I'm back in England now and I'm not planning to return to Qurhah for a while.'

Leila stared out of the window. The child which had been chasing the dog had fallen over and a woman—presumably the child's mother—was picking him up and comforting him. She realised how hopelessly ill-prepared she was to become a mother and her heart clenched. 'I'm in England too,' she said. 'In fact, I'm in London.'

She could hear so much more in that second pause. She imagined his mind working overtime as he tried to figure out what the hell she was doing in England and why she was calling him. And if he asked her outright—would she have the guts to tell him on the phone?

'What are you doing in London?'

For a moment, she didn't answer. He asked the question so casually. Did he think, with the arrogance which seemed to be second nature to all alpha males, that her desire for him was so great that she was prepared to trample over her pride in order to seek him out? Didn't he have a *clue* what she might be about to say? That their rash act of passion might have yielded this very result? 'That's what I'd like to talk to you about.'

'Where are you staying?' he asked. 'I'll come over.'

Her gaze drifted down to the traffic which was clogging the park road, knowing it would be much easier if he came here than having to negotiate her way round this strange new city. But if Gabe wanted nothing to do with this new life…then might that not complicate matters further? Why implicate him to her

retinue as the father of her baby, unless he was willing to accept that role?'

'I'm at the Granchester. But I don't want you to
come here. It's too…public.' She gripped the phone
more tightly. 'Can I come to your place?'

At the other end of the line, Gabe listened to her
hesitant words, and his eyes narrowed. It was a presumptuous question and one he would usually have
deflected. Invitations to his home were rare and *he*
was the one who did the inviting. His apartment was
his refuge. His sanctuary. It was where he went to escape. If ever he spent the night with someone, he pre-
ferred somewhere which provided him with a clearly
marked exit route. Where *he* could be the one doing
the leaving.

But Leila was different. Her royal status set her
apart from other women. It made people break rules
for her. Unwillingly, he felt the quickened beat of desire as he remembered her blue eyes and the silky tex-
ture of her olive skin. His mouth dried as he recalled
her hot, tight body. He leaned back in his chair and
stared at the ceiling. Why the hell hadn't she told him
who she really was at the time?

'This is all very mysterious,' he said. 'Do you want
to tell me what it's all about?'

'I'd rather do it in person.'

Oh, would you, my presumptuous princess? With
a flicker of irritation, Gabe waved an impatient hand
at Alice, his newly promoted assistant, who had just
stuck her head around his office door. 'Very well. I'll
send a car for you at seven.'

'No,' answered Leila flatly. 'That won't be possible.'

'Excuse me?'

'My bodyguards will not permit me to visit a man's apartment. It must be done in total secrecy. Will you be there tonight—at two a.m.?'

'Two a.m.?' His deep voice reverberated with incredulity. 'Are you out of your mind? Some of us have work to go to in the morning.'

'I'm afraid that the cover of darkness is the only solution to ensure I won't be seen, and I can't afford to be seen,' she said, a note of determination entering her voice. 'It will be best if you send the car for me then. But I need to know if you'll…if you'll be alone?'

'Yes, I'll be alone,' said Gabe coldly—and gave her the address.

Leila's heart was racing as she replaced the phone, but she couldn't shake off her feeling of apprehension—and hurt—as he cut the connection without even the politeness of a formal goodbye. Was he always this cool towards the women he'd slept with—as if he couldn't wait to put as much distance between them as possible? And how the hell was he going to react when she told him?

She told her retinue that she intended to rest for the remainder of the evening and instructed them to order themselves food from room service. Then she phoned Sara, cutting through the princess's delighted exclamations by telling her that she needed a favour.

'What kind of a favour?' asked Sara.

'Just that if my brother calls and asks if we're having a good time together, you tell him yes.'

'I think it's unlikely that your brother will call me himself,' said Sara drily. 'Is there something going on, Leila? And does that something have to do with a man?'

'How did you guess?'

'Because with most of my girlfriends, it's usually a man,' answered Sara with a wry tone. 'Don't suppose it's anyone I know?'

Leila hesitated. In a way she was wary of saying anything, but part of her wanted to blurt it out. 'Actually, you do. You used to work for him and he came to your wedding.'

There was a long silence. 'I hope you don't mean Gabe Steel?' said Sara, her voice low and disbelieving.

'That's exactly who I mean.' Leila could feel a skitter of panic washing over her skin. 'Why, what's the matter with him?'

'There's nothing the *matter* with him—that's the trouble. Just about every woman in London is or has been in love with him at some point. He's gorgeous, but he's a heartbreaker, Leila—and my advice is to stay away from him.'

It's too late for that now.

'I can't,' said Leila slowly. 'Will you cover for me, Sara?'

Sara's sigh came heaving down the phone. 'Okay, I'll cover for you—just so long as you promise me you won't do anything stupid.'

I already have, thought Leila, but she injected a breezy note into her voice.

'I promise,' she said as she put the phone down.

She could hear the sound of the room-service trolleys being trundled along the corridor towards the rooms of her retinue. Praying that their attention would be occupied by the novelty of eating Western food and that they would eat too much of it, she settled down to wait.

Shortly before ten, she allowed her servants into the room to turn down the bed and generally fuss around while she did a lot of exaggerated yawning.

The next few hours seemed to tick by with agonising slowness but Leila was too strung out to be sleepy, despite her long flight. Just before two o'clock she dressed and slipped on her raincoat and peered outside her room to find the corridor empty. With a surreptitiousness which was becoming second nature, she took the lift down into the empty foyer and walked straight outside to where Gabe's car was waiting.

Her heart was hammering as the plush vehicle whisked her through the darkened streets of London, before coming to a halt outside a looming tower of gleaming glass which overlooked the wide and glittering band of the river Thames.

And there was Gabe, waiting for her.

The pale moonlight illuminated his features, which were unsmiling and tense. As the vehicle drew to a halt she could see that he was wearing faded jeans and a sweater which hugged his honed torso and powerful arms. He looked shockingly sexy in a rock-star kind of way and that only added to Leila's feelings of discomfiture. As he bent to open the car door his eyes looked as forbidding as a frozen lake which had just been classified as unsafe.

Her mouth felt dry. Her legs were unsteady as his narrowed gaze raked over her. How was she going to go through with this?

'Hello, Leila,' he said, almost pleasantly—and she realised he was doing it again, just as he'd done on the night of the banquet. His civilised words were sending out one message while his eyes glittered out something completely different.

'Shall we go inside?'

Glass doors slid silently open to let them inside the apartment block. She was aware of a vast foyer with a jungle of elaborate plants. A man sitting reading by lamplight at a desk seemed to show surprise when he saw her walking in beside the tycoon with the dark golden hair. Or maybe she was imagining that bit.

But she certainly wasn't imagining Gabe's detached manner as they rode in one of the glass elevators towards the top of the tall building. She might as well have been travelling with a statue for all the notice he took of her, but unfortunately she wasn't similarly immune.

She tried to look somewhere—anywhere—but he filled her line of vision in his sexy, off-duty clothes. Her gaze stayed fixed determinedly on his chest for she didn't dare lift it to his face. She tried to concentrate on the steady rise and fall of his breathing instead of giving in to the darkly erotic thoughts which were crowding into her mind. He didn't want her—he couldn't have made that more clear. Yet all she could think about was the way his hands had slid round her waist when he'd still been deep inside her, the spasms dying away as he'd pumped out the last of his seed.

His seed.

The elevator stopped, the doors opened and Leila stepped out—straight into a room which momentarily took her breath away. An entire wall consisted of windows which commanded a breathtaking view of the night-time city, where stars twinkled and skyscrapers gleamed. The floors were polished and the furniture was minimalist and sleek. It was nothing like the ancient palace she called home and she felt as if she had walked into a strange new world.

For a moment she just stood and stared out of the windows. She could see the illuminated dome of St Paul's Cathedral and moonlight glittering on the river Thames. There was the sharp outline of the Shard and the pleasing circle of the London Eye. For years she had longed to come here, but never like this—because now she was seeing the famous city through the distorted lens of fear.

'Can I get you a drink?' he asked.

Leila allowed herself a moment of fantasy that this was a normal date between two people who had been lovers. How would that work? Would he open champagne and let her drink some before taking the glass from her hand and kissing her? Was that how he usually operated? Probably not at two in the morning when his night was being disturbed by a woman he was indifferent to...

For a moment she wondered what she might have done in this situation if she'd been a normal, Western woman—with all the freedoms that those women seemed to take for granted. There would have been no need for her to behave like this. Moving around under cover of darkness. Having to throw herself on the mercy of someone who didn't want her...

'No, I don't want a drink, thanks,' she said. 'That's not why I'm here.'

'Then why don't you sit down,' he suggested, 'and tell me why you are?'

She sank onto a leather sofa which was more comfortable than it looked. 'Look, there's no easy way to say this—and I know it's going to come as a shock, but I think I'm pregnant.'

For a moment Gabe didn't say a word. He couldn't. It was a long time since he had felt fear, but he felt it now. It was there in the hard beat of his heart and the icy prickle of his skin. And along with fear came anger. The sense that something was happening to him which was outside his control—and hadn't he vowed a long time ago never to let that happen to him again?

Yet on some instinctive and fundamental level, her words were not as shocking as she had suggested. Because hadn't he already guessed what she was going to say? Why else would she have pursued him like this across thousands of miles? She was a desert princess and surely someone like her wouldn't normally seek out a man who'd shown her nothing but coldness, no matter how much she had enjoyed the sex.

But none of his thoughts showed in his face. He had been a survivor for too long to react to her dramatic words—at least, not straight away. He had spent his life perfecting this cool and impenetrable mask and now was not the time to let it slip. He studied her shadowed eyes and seized on the words which offered most hope. The only hope.

'You only *think* you're pregnant?'

She nodded. 'Yes, but I'm pretty sure. I've been sick and my...'

Her words tailed off, as if she couldn't quite bring herself to say the next bit, but Gabe was in no mood to help her out—and certainly in no mood to tiptoe around her sensibilities. Because this was the woman who had disguised herself. Who had burst into his suite and come on to him without bothering to tell him who she was. She might have been a virgin but she certainly hadn't acted like one—and he was damned if he was going to let her play the shy and sensitive card now. Not when she was threatening to disrupt the ordered calm of his life. Disrupt it? She was threatening to blow it apart.

He felt a sudden flare of rage. 'Your what?' he prompted icily.

'My period is late!' she burst out, her cheeks suddenly turning red.

'But you haven't done a pregnancy test?'

'Funnily enough, no.' She bit her lip. 'It's not exactly easy for me to slip into a chemist back home to buy myself a kit. Somebody might recognise me.'

He wanted to say, *You should have thought of that before you let me strip you naked and lead you to my bed.* But he was culpable too, wasn't he? He had deflected the advances of women before and it had never been a problem. So why hadn't he sent this one on her way? Why hadn't he read any of the glaring clues which had warned him she was trouble? Had the subterfuge of her disguise and the fact that she was being pursued by bodyguards turned him on? Brought colourful fantasy into a life which was usually so cool and ordered?

'I used a condom,' he bit out.

Like a snake gathering strength before striking again, she drew her shoulders back and glared at him with angry blue eyes. 'Are you seriously suggesting that somebody other than you could be the father, Gabe?'

He remembered the way her trembling hand had circled his erection until he had been forced to push it away, afraid he might come before he was inside her. Had she inflicted some microscopic tear in the condom with those long fingernails of hers? *And had that been deliberate?*

But he pushed those thoughts away, because nothing was certain. And a man could drive himself insane if he started thinking that way.

'I'm not suggesting anything, because at the moment all we have is a hypothetical situation,' he said. 'And we're not doing anything until we have facts. There could be a million reasons why your period is late and I'm not going to waste time thinking about some nightmare scenario which might never happen.'

Nightmare scenario.

Leila flinched as his words cut into her like the nicks of a dozen tiny blades. That was all this was to him. *Remember that. Hold that thought in your mind and never forget it. A nightmare scenario.*

Had she thought that he would make everything all right? That he would sweep her into his arms as men sometimes did in films and stroke her hair, before telling her that she had no need to worry and he would take care of everything?

Maybe she had. Maybe part of her had still bought into that helpless feminine fantasy, despite everything she knew about men and the way they treated women.

'Perhaps you could go and buy a pregnancy test for me,' she suggested, staring out at the dark sky, which was punctured by tiny stars. 'Since I find the thought of braving the London shops a little too much to contemplate at the moment.'

Something small and trembling in her voice made Gabe's eyes narrow in unwilling comprehension. He wasn't used to picturing himself inside the skin of a woman—except in the most erotic sense—but he did so now. He tried to imagine this pampered princess transplanted to a foreign country, bringing with her this terrible secret. How must it feel to give such momentous news to a man who did not want to receive it?

'We're not having some do-it-yourself session,' he said flatly. 'I will make an appointment for you to see someone in Harley Street tomorrow.'

Her eyes were suddenly wide and frightened.

'But somebody might tip off the press if I am seen going to the doctor's. And my brother mustn't find out. At least, not in that way.'

'Haven't you ever heard of the Hippocratic oath?' he questioned impatiently. 'And patient confidentiality?'

Leila almost laughed. She thought that, for a man of the world, he was being remarkably naive. Or maybe he just didn't realise that royal blood always made the stakes impossibly high. It made the onlooking world act like vultures. Didn't he realise that professional codes of conduct could fall by the wayside, when a royal scoop like this offered an unimaginably high purse?

'I'll take your word for it,' she said.

Gabe watched as she reached for her handbag. She was wearing that same damned raincoat, which reminded him uncomfortably of their erotic encounter in Qurhah. For one tempting moment he entertained the thought of having sex with her again. It had been the most amazing sex of his life and he still couldn't work out why.

Because he had been the first?

Or because her touch had felt like fire on a day when his heart had been as cold as ice?

He remembered the way her long legs had parted eagerly beneath the quest of his hungry fingers. The way she had moaned when he had touched her. He could almost feel the eager warmth of her breath on his shoulder as he'd entered her, as no man had done before. Vividly, he recalled the sensation of tightness and the spots of blood on his sheets afterwards. He closed his eyes as he remembered seeing them spattered there like some kind of trophy. It had felt *primitive*, and he didn't do primitive. He did cool and calculated and reasoned because that was the only way he'd been able to survive.

Pain gnawed at his heart as he tried to regain his equilibrium, but still his body was filled with desire. Wasn't it also primitive—and natural—for a man to want to be deep inside a woman when she'd just told him she might be carrying his child?

His mouth tightened. If he pulled her into his arms and started to kiss her, she would not resist. No woman ever did. He imagined himself reacquainting himself with her scented flesh, because wouldn't that help him make some kind of sense of this bizarre situation?

'Leila,' he said, but she had stood up very quickly and was brushing her hand dismissively over the sleeve of her raincoat, in a gesture which seemed more symbolic than necessary.

'I must get back before anyone realises I've gone,' she said.

She walked across to the other side of the room, and Gabe felt the bubble of his erotic fantasy burst as she fixed him with a cool look. For a moment it almost seemed as if she had just rejected his advances—even though he hadn't actually *made* any.

'Phone me at my hotel and tell me where to meet you tomorrow,' she said. 'I will have to use Sara as a decoy again, but I'm sure I can manage it.'

'I'm sure you can,' he said with the grim air of a man whose whole world was about to change, whether he wanted it to or not.

CHAPTER FIVE

'So,' said Leila slowly. The word was tiny and meant nothing at all, but one of them had to say *something*. Something to shatter the tense, taut silence which had descended on them the moment they'd left the consulting room. Something to make Gabe move again instead of sitting there frozen, staring out of the windscreen as if he had just seen some kind of ghost.

He had brought the car to a halt in a wide, tree-lined street, and Leila was glad he'd driven away from the Harley Street clinic which had just delivered the news she had already known.

He hadn't said a thing—not a thing—but she'd noticed the way his hands had tightened around the steering wheel, and the ashen hue which had drained his face of all colour.

She was pregnant.

Very newly pregnant—but pregnant all the same.

A new life growing was beneath a heart now racing as she waited—though she wasn't really sure what she was waiting for.

She remembered Gabe's barely perceptible intake of breath as the expensively dressed consultant had delivered the results of the test. The doctor had looked at them with the benign and faintly indulgent smile he obviously reserved for this kind of situation. Probably imagining they were yet another rich young couple eager to hear what he had to say. Had he noticed the lack of a wedding ring on her finger? Did anyone actually care about that kind of thing these days? She swallowed. They certainly did in Qurhah.

She wondered if the medic had been perceptive enough to read the body language which existed between the prospective parents. Or rather, the lack of it. She and Gabe had sat upright on adjoining antique chairs facing the medic's desk, their shoulders tense. Close, yet completely distant—like two strangers who had been put into a room to hear the most intimate of information.

But that was all they were really, wasn't it?

Two strangers who had created a life out of a moment of passion.

She turned in the low sports car to glance at Gabe. She didn't know what to do. What to say or how to cope. She wanted something to make it better, but she realised that nothing could. Something unplanned and ill-advised had resulted in both their lives being changed—*and neither of them wanted this*.

The sunlight illuminated his chiselled features, casting deep shadows beneath the high slash of his cheekbones. But still he hadn't moved. His profile was utterly motionless, as if it had been carved from a piece of golden dark marble.

She knew she couldn't keep sitting there like some sort of obedient chattel, waiting for his thoughts on what had happened. She wasn't in Qurhah now. No longer did she have to play the role of subservient female. She had always longed for equality—and this was what it was supposed to be about. Taking control of her own destiny. Learning to express her own feelings instead of waiting for guidance and approval from a man.

Knotting her fingers together in a tight fist, she knew something else, too. That she didn't want this icy-eyed Englishman to feel that she had trapped him. What kind of a man was he who could sit there like a statue in the face of such news? Didn't he feel *anything*? 'Whatever happens, I'm not going to ask you for anything,' she said. 'You must understand that.'

Gabe didn't answer straight away—and not just because her accented words sounded as disjointed as if she had been speaking them in her native tongue. He had learnt when to be silent and when to speak. Once—a long time ago—he had given in to the temptation of hot-headedness. But never again. It had been the most brutal lesson and one he had never forgotten. And then, when he'd started out in advertising and was clawing his way up the slippery slope towards success, he had learnt that you should never respond until you were certain you had the right answer.

Except that this time, he couldn't see that there *was* a right answer. Only a swirling selection of options—and none of them were good. The facts were unassailable. A woman with a baby and a man who did not wish to become a father.

Who should never become a father.

He felt a dark dread begin to creep over his heart as he wondered whether history always repeated itself. Whether humans were driven by some biological imperative over which they had no control. Driven to make the same mistakes over and over again.

'Not here,' he said, his voice tight with restraint. 'I don't intend discussing something as important as this in the front seat of a car. Do up your seat belt and let's go.'

But he could see that her hands were trembling as she struggled to perform the simple action. He leaned forward to help her, and her proximity left him momentarily disorientated. The warmth radiating from her body seemed to have intensified the spicy scent of her perfume. The sunlight was bouncing off the ebony gloss of her hair and her lips looked so unbelievably kissable that he was left with the dull ache of longing inside him.

And wanting her would only complicate things. It would cloud his mind and his judgement at a time when he needed to think clearly.

Clipping in the seat belt, he quickly moved away from the temptation she presented and started up the engine.

For a while they were silent as they stop-started through the busy streets, where outside the world carried on as normal. While inside…

He shot her a glance and saw that her face looked as white as chalk and he found himself unexpectedly shocked at the sight of her physical frailty. 'Have you eaten?' he demanded.

She shook her head. 'I'm not hungry.'

'You should be. You haven't had any lunch.' And neither had he. The morning had passed in a dazed kind of blur ever since he'd met Leila at the Harley

Street clinic, where she had been dropped off by Sara, a princess who had once worked for him.

He was still remembering the look on his assistant's face this morning when he'd told her to clear his diary for the rest of the day. Surprise didn't even come close to it. He could just imagine the gossip reverberating around the building as people started second-guessing why Gabe Steel had done the unimaginable and taken an unscheduled day off work.

And when they knew? When they discovered that the man who was famous for never committing was to become a father? What then?

'You need to eat,' he said implacably.

'I don't want anything,' she said. 'I feel sick. I've felt sick for over a month.'

'Is that intended to make me feel guilty, Leila? Because you'd better know that I won't accept all the blame.' He sent out a warning toot on his horn, and the cyclist who had shot out from a side road responded with a rude gesture. 'If you hadn't come on to me in a weak moment, then we wouldn't have found ourselves in this intolerable situation.'

Wondering briefly what the weak moment had been, Leila leaned her head back against the seat as the cool venom of his words washed over her. Yet, she couldn't really condemn him for speaking the truth, could she? It *was* intolerable—and there wasn't a thing that was going to make it better. A wave of panic hit her and the now-familiar refrain echoed around in her head.

She was ruined.

Ruined.

Outside the car window, London passed by but she

barely noticed the brand-new city which should have excited her. She felt like an invisible speck of dust being blown along and she didn't know where she was going to end up. She was with a man who did not want her but was forced to be with her, because she carried his child within her belly.

'Where are you taking me?' she asked.

'To my apartment.'

She shook her head. 'I can't be seen at your apartment. My brother might find out.'

'Your brother is going to have to find out sooner or later—and this isn't about him or his reaction to what's happening. Not any more. This is about you.' *And me*, he thought reluctantly. *Me*.

Without another word he drove to his apartment and parked in the underground garage before they took the elevator to his apartment. The rooms seemed both strange yet familiar and Leila felt disorientated as she walked inside. As if she was a different person from the one who had arrived here in the early hours of this morning.

But she was.

Yesterday nothing had been certain and there had still been an element of hope in her heart, no matter how misplaced. But with the doctor's diagnosis, that hope had gone and nothing would ever be the same. Never again would she simply be Leila, the princess sister of the Sultan. Soon she would be Leila, the mother of an illegitimate child—a baby fathered by the tycoon Gabe Steel.

The man who had never wanted to see her again.

She tried to imagine her brother's fury when she found out but it was hard to picture the full extent of his predictable rage. Would he strip her of her title? Banish her from the only land and home she had ever known? And if he did—what then? She tried to imagine supporting herself and a tiny baby. How would she manage that when she'd never even *held* a baby?

She was so preoccupied with the tumult of her thoughts that it took her a few minutes to realise that Gabe had left her alone in his stark sitting room. He returned a little while later with his suit jacket removed and the sleeves of his shirt rolled up. She noticed his powerful forearms with their smattering of dark golden hair and remembered the way he had slid them around her naked waist. And wasn't that a wildly inappropriate thing to remember at a time like this?

'I've made us something to eat,' he said. 'Come through to the dining room.'

His words made Leila's sense of disorientation increase because she came from a culture where men didn't cook. Where they had nothing to do with the preparation of food—unless you counted hunting it down in the desert and then killing it.

She told herself that he wasn't listening to what she'd said—and she'd said she wasn't hungry. But it seemed rude to sit here on her own while he ate and so she followed him into the dining room.

This was not a comfortable room either. He was clearly a fan of minimalism, and the furniture looked like something you might find in the pages of an architectural magazine. Tea and sandwiches sat on a table constructed from dull metal, around which was a circle of hard, matching chairs. The table sat beneath the harsh glare of the skylight, which made Leila think she was about to be interrogated.

And maybe that wasn't such a bad idea. She certainly had a few questions she needed to put to the man now pushing a plate of food towards her.

She held up the palm of her hand. 'I don't—'

'Just try,' he interrupted. 'Is that too much to ask, Leila?'

The hard timbre of his voice had softened into something which sounded almost gentle and the way he said her name suddenly made her feel horribly vulnerable. Or maybe she was imagining that. Maybe she was looking for crumbs of comfort when all he was doing was being practical. She realised that she felt weak and that if she didn't look after herself she would get weaker still. And she couldn't afford to do that.

So she ate most of the sandwich and drank a cup of jasmine tea before pushing away her plate. Leaning back against the hard iron chair, she crossed her arms defensively over her chest and studied him.

She drew in a deep breath. 'You can rest assured that I don't expect anything from you, Gabe. You've made your feelings absolutely plain. That afternoon was a mistake—we both know that. We were never intended to be together and this…this *baby* doesn't have to change that. I want you to know that you're free to walk away. And that I can manage on my own—'

'What are you planning to do?' The question fired from his mouth like a blistering fusillade of shots. 'To get rid of it?'

The accusation appalled her almost as much as the thought that he should think her capable of such an action, and Leila glared at him. *He doesn't know you*, she realised bitterly. *He doesn't even* like *you*.

'How dare you make a suggestion like that?' she

said, unable to keep the anger from her voice. 'I'm not ready to be a mother. I'm not sure I ever wanted to *be* a mother, but it seems that fate has decided otherwise. And I will accept that fate,' she added fiercely. 'I will have this baby and I will look after him—or her. And nothing and no one will stop me.'

Some of the tension had left him, but his mouth was still unsmiling as his gaze raked over her face. 'And just how are you planning to go about that?' he demanded. 'You who are a protected and pampered princess who can't move around freely unless under cover of darkness. What are you going to tell your brother? And how are you intending to support yourself when the child comes?'

She wished there were some place to look other than at his eyes, because they were distracting her. They were reminding her of how soft and luminous they'd been when he had held her in his arms. They were making her long for things she could never have. Things like love and warmth and closeness. A man to cradle her and tell her that everything was going to be all right.

But she didn't dare shift her gaze away from his, because wouldn't that be a sign of a weakness? A weakness she dared not show. Not to him. Not to her brother. Not to anyone. Because from here on in she must be strong.

Strong.

'I have jewellery I can sell,' she said.

His smile was faint. 'Of course you do.'

She heard the sardonic note in his voice. Another *rich princess* reference, she thought bitterly. 'Things my mother left me,' she added.

'And how do you propose getting your hands on this jewellery?' he questioned. 'Are you planning to take a trip to Qurhah and smuggle it out of the safe? Or perhaps you're thinking of asking your brother to mail it to you?'

'I could probably...I might be able to get one of my servants to get it to me,' she said unconvincingly. 'It would be risky, of course, but I'm sure it could be doable.'

Gabe gave a short laugh. Of all the women who could have ended up carrying his baby, it had to be her. A spoiled little rich girl who just snapped her beautiful fingers and suddenly money appeared. Did she really think it was going to be that easy?

His customary cool composure momentarily deserting him, he leaned across the table towards her. 'Do you really think your brother will be amenable to you taking funds out of the country to support an illegitimate baby?'

Her face seemed to crumple at the word, and Gabe felt a brief twist of regret that he had spoken to her so harshly. But she needed to confront the truth—no matter how unpalatable she found it.

'You have to face facts, Leila,' he said. 'And you're not going to find this easy. At some point you're going to have to tell your brother what's happened.' He saw the way her eyelids slid down to conceal the sudden brightness of her eyes, the thick lashes forming two ebony arcs which feathered against her skin. 'Have you thought about what his reaction might be?'

'I have thought of little else!'

'So what are you planning to tell him?'

The lashes fluttered open and the look in her eyes

was defiant, though the faint tremble of her lips less so. 'Oh, I won't mention your name, if that's what you're worried about.'

'I am not frightened of your brother, Leila. And neither am I denying what happened—no matter how much I might now regret it.' His mouth hardened. 'I'm asking what you are intending to tell Murat.'

She didn't answer for a moment and when she did, her voice was heavy. 'I guess I'm going to have to tell him the truth.'

'Or your unique version of the truth?' he questioned wryly. 'Won't the Sultan think that his sister's innocence has been compromised by a man with enough experience to have known better? It might suit your purpose—and his—to convince him that you were taken advantage of by an Englishman with something of a reputation where the opposite sex is concerned. Mightn't it be more acceptable for him to think of you as a victim rather than a predator?'

'I'm no victim, Gabe!' she flared back. 'And I'm no predator either, no matter how much it suits *you* to think that. I certainly didn't plan to seduce you—I was a virgin, for heaven's sake! I just…just gave into the "chemistry" you were talking about. And you certainly didn't seem to be objecting at the time.'

'No, you're right. I didn't put up much in the way of a fight.' His face tightened—as if her words were taking him some place he didn't want to go. 'But your brother is going to wonder when and where this great love affair of ours took place.'

She flushed. 'Obviously, he doesn't know that I came to your hotel room.'

'Actually, you came *in* my hotel room,' he reminded

her sardonically. 'Don't forget that part of the story, Leila—because it's probably the best part of all.'

Her flush deepened as his words brought back memories of the way it had been that day. The way he had kissed her and told her she was beautiful. In those few brief and glorious moments, she'd thought she'd found her heart's desire. For a short while she had felt as perfect as it was possible to feel.

But those feelings were in the past and they had been nothing but fantasy. All that was left was the brittle reality of the present—so why torture herself by remembering something which had been so fleeting?

'That's irrelevant,' she said. 'And I'm not scared of my brother.' But then some of her bravado left her. Tiredly, she lifted up her hands and buried her face in them as the warm darkness enveloped her like a welcoming cloak.

'Leila?' His voice was suddenly soft. 'Are you *cry-ing*?'

'No, I am *not*!' she said fiercely, but she kept her face hidden all the same.

'Then look at me,' he commanded.

Rebellion flared inside her. She didn't *want* to look at him because, although there were no tears, she was afraid of what he might be able to read in her eyes. She didn't want to expose her sense of deflation and de-feat. The liberated woman she'd yearned to be seemed to have slipped away into the shadows and was no-where to be seen. And she had no one to blame but herself. She had gone to a *known playboy's* bedroom and let him kiss her. Why had she thought that having sex with a total stranger was somehow *empowering*?

'I have a solution,' he said.

His words broke into her thoughts. She lowered her hands but her head remained bent—as if she had found something uniquely fascinating to look at on the dark denim of her jeans. 'You have a magic wand with the power to turn back time, do you?'

'Unfortunately, I'm clean out of magic wands, so it looks like I'll just have to marry you instead.'

At this, her head jerked up, her gaze meeting his in disbelief. 'What?'

'You heard. And you're clever enough to realise it's the only option. I have no choice, other than to make you my wife—because I can see it would be intolerably cruel to let a woman like you face this on your own.' His eyes glittered like ice. 'Because you are not on your own. I share equal responsibility for what has happened, although you are a princess while I am…'

His face grew taut and Leila saw the sudden flare of pain which had darkened his grey eyes.

'You're what?' she prompted breathlessly.

For a moment he said nothing. A sudden darkness passed over his face, but just as quickly it was gone. The billionaire tycoon was back in control.

'It doesn't matter. For obvious reasons, this child cannot be born illegitimate. You will not need to hide your head in shame, Leila. I didn't ever want to be a husband.' His cool eyes flashed silver. 'Or a father. But as you say—fate seems to have decided otherwise. And I will accept that fate. We will be married as soon as possible.'

It should have been the dream solution but to Leila it felt like no such thing. She didn't want to marry a man who looked as if he were destined for a trip to the gallows, or to live with the realisation that she had trapped him into a life he didn't want. She couldn't imagine ever bonding with this icy *stranger*.

'I won't do it,' she said stubbornly. 'I won't tie myself to a man who doesn't want me. And you can't make me marry you.'

'You think not?' The smile he gave did not meet his eyes. 'You'd be surprised what I can do if I set my mind to it—but I'm hoping that we can come to some kind of *amicable* agreement. These are the only terms I am offering and I'd advise you to accept them. Because you're not really in any position to object. Your brother will disown you if you don't and I doubt whether you have a clue how to look after yourself. Not in a strange city without your servants and bodyguards to accede to your every whim. You cannot subject a baby to a life like that and I won't allow you to, because this is my baby too. You will marry me, Leila, because there is no alternative.'

CHAPTER SIX

LEILA STARED INTO the full-length mirror at someone who looked just like her. Who moved just like her. A woman who was startlingly familiar yet who seemed like a total stranger.

She was eight weeks pregnant by a man who didn't love her and today was her wedding day.

She glanced around the luxury hotel room to which she would never return. Her suitcases had already been collected by Gabe's driver and taken to his riverside apartment, which was to be her new home after she became his wife. She thought about the bare rooms and the minimalist decor which awaited her. She thought about the harsh, clear light which flooded in from the river. As if such a soulless place as that could ever be described as home!

He had asked her to be his bride, yet he had made her feel as if she was an unwanted piece of baggage he had been forced to carry. She had eventually—and reluctantly—agreed with him that marriage seemed to be the only sensible solution, when his phone had begun to ring. *And he had answered it!* He had left her sitting there as if she'd been invisible while he had conducted a long and boring business call right in front of her. It had not been a good omen—or an encouraging sign about the way he treated women.

Inside she had been seething, but what could she do? She could hardly storm out onto the unknown streets of London—or rush back to the safety of Qurhah, where nobody would want a princess who had brought shame onto her family name. She had felt trapped—and her heart had sunk like a heavy stone which had been dropped into a river. Was she destined to feel trapped for the rest of her days, no matter where in the world she lived?

Her reflected image stared back at her and she regarded it almost objectively. Her bridal dress of cobalt-blue was sleek and concealing and the hotel hairdresser had woven crimson roses into her black hair. She had refused to wear white on principle. It hadn't seemed appropriate in the circumstances. Much too romantic a gesture for such an occasion as this— because what was romantic about an expectant bride being taken reluctantly by a man who had no desire to be married to her?

Yet didn't some stupid part of her wish that it could all be different? Didn't she wish she were floating along on a happy pink cloud, the way brides were *supposed* to do? Maybe all those books and films she'd devoured during her lonely life at the palace had left their mark on her after all. She had no illusions about men or marriage, but that didn't stop her from wanting the dream—like some teenager who still believed that anything was possible.

But at least this was to be a quiet wedding. And a quick wedding—which had presented more of a problem.

The three-week wait required by English law had not been practical for a couple in their situation. As a desert princess, she could not live with Gabe and she had no desire to spend weeks in limbo at the Granchester Hotel, no matter how luxurious her suite there. Short of flying to Vegas, the only alternative was to get married in the Qurhahian Embassy in London—for which she needed her brother's permission. And she hadn't wanted to ask him, because she hadn't wanted to tell him why she needed to marry the Englishman in such a rush.

Yet she'd known she was going to have to break the news to Murat some time, hadn't she? She'd known she was going to have to tell him she was having Gabe's baby—so how could he refuse to grant her use of the embassy? She knew—and he knew—that the niece or nephew of the Sultan could not be born outside wedlock.

It had been the most difficult conversation of her life—not helped by the fact that it had been conducted by telephone. Her nervous stammering had been halted by Gabe taking the phone from her and quietly telling the Sultan that he intended to marry her. She wasn't sure what Murat actually said in response because Gabe had just stood there and listened to what sounded like an angry tirade thundering down the line.

But the Englishman had stood his ground and, after calmly reasserting his determination to take her as his bride, had handed the phone back to Leila.

Beneath Gabe's grey gaze, she had explained to Murat that while she would prefer to do this with his blessing, she was perfectly prepared to do it without.

Such a wait would, of course, mean living with a man who was not her husband.

The Sultan had sounded shocked—as much by her attitude as by her words—for she was aware that few people ever openly defied him. But unexpectedly, his voice had softened and for a moment he had sounded just like the Murat she'd thought no longer existed. The one she'd seen all those years ago, after their mother had died. When for once he had let down his guard and Leila had sobbed in his arms until there were no tears left to cry. And afterwards she'd noticed his own damp cheeks and seen the grief which had ravaged his dark face.

That was the only time in her life she had seen her brother showing emotion until now, when he asked her a question which came out of nowhere.

'And do you love him, Leila?' he had asked her quietly. 'This man Gabe Steel.'

Leila had closed her eyes and walked to the far end of the room, knowing that a lie was the only acceptable answer. A lie would make Murat leave them alone. A lie would confer an odd kind of blessing on this strange marriage.

'Yes,' she had answered in a low voice, glad that Gabe was not within earshot. 'Yes, I love him.'

And that had been that. Blessing conferred. They were given permission to use the embassy although Murat told her he would not be attending the nuptials himself.

In fact, the ceremony was to have only two witnesses—Sara and her husband, Suleiman, who had also known Leila since she had been a child. A relatively informal lunch following the ceremony was to be their only celebration. Time had been too tight to arrange anything else, although Gabe told her that a bigger party for his colleagues and friends could be arranged later, if she was so inclined.

Was she? She didn't know any of his colleagues or friends. She knew hardly anything about him—and in truth he seemed to want it to stay that way. It was as if the man she was marrying was an undiscovered country—one which she had suddenly found herself inhabiting without use of a compass. She was used to men who told women little—or nothing—but this was different. She was having his baby, for heaven's sake—and surely that gave her some sort of *right* to know.

On the eve of their wedding, they had been eating an early dinner in the Granchester's award-winning rooftop restaurant when she'd plucked up enough courage to ask him a few questions.

'You haven't mentioned your parents, Gabe.'

His expression had been as cold as snow. 'That's because they're dead. I'm an orphan, Leila—just like you.'

The cool finality in his tone had been intimidating but she wasn't going to give up that easily. She had put down her glass of fizzy water and looked him squarely in the eyes.

'What about brother or sisters?'

'Sadly, there's none. Just me.' The smile which had followed this statement had been mocking. 'Tell me, did you bring your camera to England with you?'

The change of subject had been so abrupt that Leila had blinked at him in confusion. 'No. I left Qurhah in such a hurry that my camera was the last thing on my mind.'

'Pity. I thought it might have given you something to do.'

'I'm going to buy myself a new one,' she said defensively.

'Good.'

It was only afterwards that she realised he had very effectively managed to halt her line in questioning, with the adroitness of a man who was a master of concealment.

But now was not the moment to dwell on all the things which were missing from their relationship, because Sara had arrived to accompany her to the embassy for the wedding and Leila knew she must push her troubled thoughts aside. She must pin a bright smile to her lips and be prepared to play the part expected of her. Because if Sara guessed at her deep misgivings about the marriage, then mightn't she try to talk her out of it?

They embraced warmly and Sara's smile was soft as she pulled away and studied her. 'You look utterly exquisite, Leila,' she said. 'I hope Gabe knows what a lucky man he is.'

Somehow, Leila produced an answering smile. Lucky? She knew Sara had guessed the truth—that she was newly pregnant with Gabe's baby. But Sara wasn't aware that the thought of having a baby didn't scare her nearly as much as the fact that she was marrying a man who seemed determined to remain a stranger to her. She thought of his shuttered manner. The way he had batted back her questions as if she had no right to ask them. How could she possibly cope with living with such a man?

Yet as she made a final adjustment to her flowered headdress she felt a little stab of determination. Couldn't she break through the emotional barriers which Gabe Steel had erected around his heart? She had come this far—too far—to be dismissed as if what she wanted didn't matter. Because it *did* matter. *She* mattered. And no matter how impossible it seemed, she knew what was top of her wish-list. She wanted Gabe to be close to her and their baby. She'd had enough of families who lived their lives in separate little boxes—she'd done that all her life. Sometimes what you wanted didn't just *happen*—you had to reach out and grab it for yourself. And grab it she would.

'Let's hope he does,' she said with a smile as she picked up her bouquet.

But her new-found determination couldn't quite dampen down her flutter of nerves as the car took her and Sara to Grosvenor Square, where Gabe was standing on the steps waiting for her.

She thought how formidably gorgeous he looked as he came forward to greet her. Toweringly tall in a charcoal suit which contrasted with the dark gold of his hair, he seemed all power and strength. She told herself she wouldn't have been human if her body hadn't begun to tremble with excitement in response to him.

But he was only standing there because he had no choice.

Because she was carrying his baby.

That was all.

'Hello, Leila,' he said.

Her apprehension diminished a little as she saw the momentary darkening of his quicksilver eyes. 'Hello, Gabe,' she answered.

'You look…incredible.'

The compliment took her off-guard and so did the way he said it. Her fingers fluttered upwards to check the positioning of the crimson flowers in her hair. 'Do I?'

Gabe read the uncertainty in her eyes and knew that he could blot it out with a kiss. But he didn't want to kiss her. Not now and not in public. Not with all these damned embassy officials hovering around, giving him those narrow-eyed looks of suspicion, as they'd been doing ever since he'd arrived. He wondered if they resented their beautiful princess marrying a man from outside their own culture. Or whether they guessed this was a marriage born of necessity, rather than of love.

Love.

He hoped his exquisite bride wasn't entertaining any fantasies about love—and maybe he needed to spell that out for her. To start as he meant to go on. With the truth. To tell her that he was incapable of love. That he had ice for a heart and a dark hole for a soul. That he broke women's hearts without meaning to.

His mouth hardened.

Would he break hers, too?

CHAPTER SEVEN

THE MARRIAGE CEREMONY was conducted in both
Qurhahian and English, and Gabe reflected more than
once that the royal connection might have intimidated
many men. But he was not easily intimidated and essentially it was the same as any other wedding he'd
ever been to. He and Leila obediently repeated words
which had been written by someone else. He slid a
gleaming ring onto her finger and they signed a register, although his new wife's signature was embel-
lished with a royal crest stamped into a deep blob of
scarlet wax.

She put the pen down and rose gracefully from the
seat, but as he took her hand in his he could feel her
trembling and he found his fingers tightening around
hers to give her an encouraging squeeze.

'You are now man and wife,' said the official, his
robed figure outlined against the indigo and golden
hues of the Qurhahian flag.

Sara and Suleiman smilingly offered their congratulations as soft sounds of Qurhahian *Takht* music
began to play. Servants appeared as if by clockwork,
bearing trays of the national drink—a bittersweet
combination of pomegranate juice mixed with zest

of lime. After this they were all led into a formal dining room, where a wedding breakfast awaited them, served on a table festooned with crimson roses and golden goblets studded with rubies.

Leila found herself feeling disorientated as she sat down opposite Suleiman and began to pick at the familiar Qurhahian food which was presented to her. The enormity of all that had happened to her should have been enough to occupy her thoughts during the meal. But all she could think about was the powerful presence of her new husband and to wonder what kind of future lay ahead.

Who *was* Gabe Steel? she wondered as she stabbed at a sliver of mango with her fork. She listened to him talking to Sara about the world of advertising and then slipping effortlessly into a conversation about oil prices with Suleiman. He was playing his part perfectly, she thought. Nobody would ever have guessed that this was a man who had effectively been shotgunned into marriage.

He must have sensed her watching him, for he suddenly reached out his hand and laid it on top of hers, and Leila couldn't prevent an involuntary shiver of pleasure in response. It had been weeks since he'd touched her, and she revelled in the feeling of his warm flesh against hers—but the gesture felt more dutiful than meaningful. She couldn't stop noticing the way Suleiman and Sara were with each other. The way they hung off the other's every word and finished each other's sentences. She felt a tug of wistfulness in her heart. Their marriage was so obviously a love-match and it seemed to mock the emptiness of the relationship she shared with Gabe.

She turned to find his cool grey gaze on hers.

'Enjoying yourself?' he said.

She wondered what he would say if she told him the truth. That she felt blindsided with bewilderment about the future and fearful of being married to a man who gave nothing away.

But Leila was a princess who had been taught never to show her feelings in public. She could play her part as well as he was playing his. She could make her reply just as non-committal as the cool question he'd asked.

'It's been a very interesting day,' she conceded.

Unexpectedly, he gave a low laugh—as if her un-emotional response had pleased him. He bent his lips to her ear. 'I think we might leave soon, don't you?'

'I think that might be acceptable,' she said, swallowing in an effort to shift the sudden dryness in her throat.

'I think so too,' he agreed. 'So let's say goodbye to our guests and go.'

The unmistakeable intent which edged his words made Leila's heart race with excitement. But hot on that flare of anticipation came apprehension, because the sex they'd shared that afternoon in Qurhah now seemed like a distant dream.

What would it be like to make love with him again after everything that had happened? What if this time it was a disappointment—what then? Because she suspected that a man as experienced as Gabe would not tolerate a wife who didn't excite him. Wasn't that why men in the desert kept harems—to ensure that their sexual appetites were always gratified? Wasn't it said in Qurhah that no one woman could ever satisfy a man?

Her heart was pounding erratically as he led her outside to his waiting car. Leila slid inside and the quicksilver gleam of his eyes was brighter than her new platinum wedding ring as he joined her on the back seat. Suddenly, she imagined what her life might have been like if Gabe had refused to marry her, as he could so easily have done. She imagined her brother's fury and her country's sense of shame and she felt a stab of gratitude towards the Englishman with the hard body and the dark golden hair.

'Thank you,' she said quietly.

'For what?'

'Oh, you know.' She kept her voice light. 'For saving me from a life of certain ruin—that sort of thing.'

He gave a short laugh. 'I did it because I had to. No other reason. Don't start thinking of me as some benign saviour with nothing but noble intentions in his heart. Because that man does not exist. I'm a cold-hearted bastard, Leila—or so your sex have been telling me all my adult life. And since that is unlikely to change, it's better that I put you straight right from the start. The truth might hurt, but sometimes it's a kinder pain than telling lies. Do you understand?'

'Sure,' said Leila, her voice studiedly cool as her fingers dug into the wedding bouquet which she would have liked to squash against his cold and impassive face. Couldn't the truth have waited for another day? Couldn't he have allowed her one day of fantasy before the harshness of reality hit them? But men only did that kind of mushy stuff in films. Never in real life.

'But understand something else,' he added softly.

'That my lack of emotion does not affect my desire for you. I have thought of nothing else but you and although I badly want to kiss you, you'll have to wait a little while longer. Because while I'm fairly confident the press haven't got hold of this story, I can't guarantee that the paparazzi aren't lying in wait outside my apartment. And we don't want them picturing you getting out of the car looking completely ravaged, do we, my beautiful blue-eyed princess?'

'We certainly don't,' said Leila, still reeling from his cold character assessment—followed by those contrasting heated words of desire.

But there were no paparazzi outside the apartment—just the porter who'd been sitting behind the desk the first time she'd been here and who now smiled as they walked into the foyer.

'Congratulations, Mr Steel,' the man said, with the tone of someone who realised that normal deference could be relaxed on such a day. 'Aren't you going to carry the lady over the threshold?'

Gabe gave a ghost of a smile as he stared down into Leila's eyes. 'My wife doesn't like heights,' he said. 'Do you, darling?'

'Oh, I absolutely loathe them,' she said without a flicker of reaction.

But irrationally, she felt a stab of disappointment as they rode upstairs in the elevator. Despite what he'd said in the car, it wouldn't have hurt him to play the part of adoring groom in front of the porter, would it? They said that men fantasised about sex—well, didn't he realise that women did the same thing about weddings, no matter how foolish that might be?

'Why are you frowning?' he questioned as the door of his apartment swung silently shut behind them.

'You wouldn't understand.'

Tilting her chin with his finger, he put her eyes on a collision course with his. 'Try me.'

She tried all right. She tried to ignore the sizzle of her skin as he touched her, but it was impossible. Even that featherlight brush of his finger on her chin was distracting. Everything about him was distracting. Yet his grey eyes were curious—as if he was genuinely interested in her reasons. And wasn't that as good a start as any to this bizarre marriage?

So start by telling him what it is you want. He has just advocated the use of truth, so tell him. Tell him the truth. She held his gaze. 'If you must know, I quite liked the idea of being carried over the threshold.'

Dark eyebrows arched. 'I thought you might find it hypocritical under the circumstances.'

'Maybe it is.' She shrugged. 'It's just that I've never been carried anywhere before—well, presumably I was, as a baby. But not as an adult and never by a man. And this might be the only stab at it I get.'

'Oh, I see,' he said. He took the bouquet from her hand and placed it on a nearby table. 'Would carrying you to bed compensate for my shocking omission as a bridegroom?'

She met the glitter of his eyes and excitement began to whisper over her skin. He was flirting with her, she realised. And maybe she ought to flirt right back. 'I don't know,' she said doubtfully. 'We could try it out and see.'

He gave a flicker of a smile as he bent and slid one arm under her knees, picking her up with an ease which didn't surprise her. Leila might have been tall for a woman but Gabe made her feel tiny. He made her feel all soft and yearning. He made her feel things she had no right to feel. Her arms fastened themselves around his neck as he carried her along a long, curving corridor into his bedroom.

She'd only been in here once before to unpack her clothes and find a home for her shoes. But then, as now—she had been slightly overwhelmed by the essential *masculinity* of the room. A vast bed was the centrepiece—and everything else seemed to be concealed. Wardrobes and drawers were tucked away out of sight, and she could see why. Any kind of clutter would have detracted from the floor-to-ceiling windows which commanded such a spectacular view over the river.

She tried to imagine bringing a baby into this stark environment and felt curiously exposed as he set her down on her gleaming wedding shoes.

'Won't we…be seen?' she questioned, her gaze darting over his shoulder as he began to unfasten her dress.

'The windows are made specially so that people can't see in from the outside,' he murmured. 'Like car windows. So there's no need to worry.'

But Leila had plenty to worry about. The first time they'd done this, there had been no time to think. This time around and she'd done nothing *but* think. How many women had stood where she had stood? Women who were far more experienced than she was. Who would have known where to touch him and how to please him.

His fingers had loosened some of the fastenings,

and the dress slid down to her waist, leaving her torso bare. She felt *exposed*. And vulnerable. He bent his head to kiss her shoulder, but she couldn't help stiffening as he traced the tip of his tongue along the arrowing bone.

He drew his head away from her and frowned. 'What's wrong?'

'I don't know. This feels so...' Awkwardly, her words trailed off. She could pretend that nothing was wrong but she remembered what he'd said in the car. That the truth could hurt, but lies could hurt even more. And if she kept piling on layer after layer of fake stuff, her life would be reduced to one big falsehood. In a marriage such as theirs—wasn't the truth the only way to safeguard her sanity? 'So cold-blooded,' she said.

'You're nervous?'

'I guess so.'

'You weren't nervous last time.'

'I know.' She licked her lips. 'But last time felt different.'

'How?'

'Because we weren't thinking or analysing. There was no big agenda. No frightening future yawning ahead of us. It just...happened. Almost like it was meant to happen.'

For a moment she wondered if she'd said too much. Whether that final sentence had sounded like the hopeless yearning of an impressionable young woman. The truth was all very well, but she didn't want to come over as *needy*.

He stroked his hand down over her cheek and moved it round to her neck. His grey eyes narrowed and then suddenly he dug his fingers into her hair and brought his mouth down on hers in a crushing kiss.

It was the kiss which changed everything. The kiss which ignited the fire. All the pent-up emotion she'd kept inside for weeks was now set free. And suddenly it didn't matter that Gabe had warned her about having ice for a heart because, for now at least, he was all heat and flame and maybe that was enough to melt him.

She clung to him as his mouth explored hers, and he began to pull the pins from her hair. Silken strands spilled down around her shoulders, one after another. She could feel them tickling her back as they fell. Cool air was washing over her skin as he unclipped her bra and her breasts sprang free.

He stopped kissing her and stood for a moment, just observing her. And then, very deliberately, he reached out and cupped a breast in the palm of his hand, his eyes not leaving her face as he rotated his thumb against the nipple.

'Gabe,' she said indistinctly.

'What?' The thumb was replaced by the brush of his lips as he bent his head to the super-sensitive nub, and Leila closed her eyes as pleasure washed over her. Her senses felt raw and alive—as if he'd just rehabilitated them from a long sleep. She reached towards his shirt buttons, but the effort of undoing even one seemed too arduous when his hand was skimming so possessively over her waist and touching the bare skin there.

With a low laugh which sounded close to a growl, he freed the last fastenings of her dress and let it slide to the ground.

Stepping out from the circle of concertinaed silk, she looked up at his dark face, and something about his expression made her heart miss a beat. All her doubts and fears were suddenly replaced by something infinitely more dangerous. Something which had happened the last time she'd been in this situation. Because wasn't there something about Gabe Steel which called out to her on a level she didn't really understand? Something which made her feel powerful and vulnerable all at the same time.

He was a cool English billionaire who could have just thrown her to the wolves. Who could have rejected his child and made her face the consequences on her own. But he had done no such thing. He had been prepared to shoulder the heavy burden of responsibility she had placed upon his shoulders. Gabe Steel was not a bad man, she decided. He might be a very elusive and secretive one—but he was capable of compassion. And wasn't she now better placed than any other female on the planet to discover more about a person who had captivated her from the start? Couldn't she do that?

Her torpor suddenly left her as she reached towards his shirt and began to slide the buttons from their confinement. Her confidence grew as she felt his body grow tense. She could hear nothing but the laboured sound of his breathing as she opened up his shirt and feasted her eyes on the perfection of the golden skin beneath.

Bending her head, she flickered her tongue at his tight, salty nipple and she felt a sharp thrill as she heard him groan. She had never undressed a man before—but how difficult could it be? She tugged the charcoal jacket from his shoulders and let it fall on top of her discarded wedding dress. The shirt followed— so that now he was completely bare-chested, like those men she'd seen fighting for coins in one of the provincial market squares outside Simdahab.

Undoing the top button of his trousers, she was momentarily daunted by the hardness beneath the fine cloth, which made unzipping him awkward. But his fingers covered hers, and he guided her hand down over the rocky ridge, and Leila's heartbeat soared, because that shared movement felt so gloriously intimate.

With growing confidence, she dealt with his socks and shoes—and he returned the favour by easing her out of her panties and stockings.

Before long, they were both completely naked, standing face to face next to the bed. His hands were splayed over her bottom and her breasts were brushing against his chest. She could feel his erection nudging her belly and the answering wetness of her sex as she wrapped her arms around his neck.

'Are you sure we can't be seen?' she whispered.

'Why, is that your secret fantasy?' he questioned, pushing her down onto the soft mattress. 'People watching and seeing what a *naughty* princess you can be?'

Leila said nothing as his mouth moved to her neck and he moved his hand between her legs. She closed her eyes and tried to concentrate on the stroking movement of his fingers. But even intense pleasure could not completely obliterate the sudden troubled skitter of her thoughts. Was this what playboy lovers enjoyed most, she wondered—to share fantasies? Didn't he realise that she was still too much of a novice to have any real fantasies?

His eyes were dark as he moved over her, but she could see the sudden tautness of his mouth. She wondered if he was wishing that this were just uncomplicated sex. That he was not tied to her for the foreseeable future, and that there was not a baby on the way.

'Is something *wrong*?' she whispered.

'Wrong?' he echoed unsteadily. 'Are you out of your mind? I'm just savouring every delicious moment. Because for the first time in my life I don't have to worry about contraception. I'll be able to feel my bare skin inside you—and it's a very liberating feeling.'

His description sounded more mechanical than affectionate but Leila told herself to be grateful for his honesty. At least he wasn't coating his words with false sentiment and filling her with false hopes. And why spoil this moment by wishing for the impossible, instead of enjoying every incredible second?

Tipping her head back, she revelled in the sensation of what he was doing to her.

The way his lips were moving over hers.

The way his fingers played so distractingly over her skin, setting up flickers of reaction wherever they alighted.

The way he...

'Oh, Gabe,' she breathed as she felt him brushing intimately against her.

Slowly, he eased himself inside her, the almost-entry of his moist tip followed by one long, silken thrust. For a moment he stilled and allowed her body to adjust to him.

'I'm not hurting you?' he questioned.

Hurting her? That was the last thing he was doing. She was aware that he fitted her as perfectly as the last piece of a jigsaw puzzle which had just been slotted into place. She had never felt as complete as she did in that moment, and wouldn't the cool Gabe Steel be horrified if he knew she was thinking that way?

'No,' she breathed, shaking her head. 'You're not hurting me.'

'And does it feel—different?'

She met the smoky question in his eyes. 'Different?'

'Because of the baby?'

Would it terrify him if she told him that yes, it did? That it felt unbelievably profound to have his flesh inside her, while their combined flesh grew deep in her belly. Much too profound for comfort. She pressed her lips against the dark rasp of his jaw.

'I don't really have enough experience for comparison,' she whispered.

He tilted her face upwards so that all she could see was the gleam of his silver gaze. 'That sounds like a blatant invitation to provide you with a little more.'

'D-does it?'

'Mmm. So I think I'd better do just that, don't you?'

She gasped as he began a slow, sweet rhythm inside her. Her fingertips slid greedily over the silken skin which cloaked his moving muscles. Eagerly, she began to explore the contours of his body—the power of his rock-hard legs and the taut globes of his buttocks.

She felt part of him.

All of him.

She felt in that moment as if anything was possible.

'Gabe,' she moaned, her body beginning to tense.

His mouth grazed hers. 'Tell me.'

'I c-can't.'

'Tell me,' he urged again.

'Oh. *Oh!*'

Gabe felt her buck beneath him in helpless rapture. His mouth came down hard on hers as her back arched, his fingers tightening over her narrow hips. He became aware of the softness of her belly as he pressed against her and then he let go—spilling his seed into her with each long and exquisite thrust.

For a while he was aware of nothing other than the fading spasms deep within his body and a sense of emptiness and of torpor. Automatically, he rolled away onto the other side of the bed where he lay on top of the rumpled sheet and sucked mouthfuls of air back into his lungs. His eyelids felt as if they'd been weighted with lead. He wanted to sleep. To sleep for a hundred years. To hold on to a sensation which felt peculiarly close to contentment.

But old habits died hard and he fought the feeling and the warm place which was beckoning to him, automatically replacing it with ice-cold logic. All he was experiencing was the stupefying effect of hormones as his body gathered up its resources to make love to her again. It was sex, that was all. Surprisingly good sex—but nothing more than that. How could it ever be more than that?

Meeting her bright blue gaze, he flickered her a non-commital smile.

'What a perfect way to begin a honeymoon,' he drawled.

CHAPTER EIGHT

IT WAS A honeymoon of sorts.

Leila supposed that some people might even have considered it a successful honeymoon. With time and money at his disposal, Gabe set about showing her a London she'd only ever seen in films or books—and the famous city came to life before her eyes.

They visited Buckingham Palace and the famous Tower where two young princes had once been imprisoned. They took a ride on a double-decker bus, which thrilled Leila since she'd never been on public transport before. They went to galleries and museums and saw some of the long-running West End shows.

He showed her a 'secret' London too—a side to the city known only to the people who lived in it. Restaurants with flower-filled courtyards which were tucked away behind industrial grey streets and intimate concert halls where he took her to hear exquisite classical music.

And when they weren't sightseeing they were having sex. Lots of it. Inventive, imaginative and mind-blowing sex, which left her gasping and breathless with pleasure every time. She told herself she was lucky—and when she was kissing her gorgeous new husband, she *felt* lucky.

But while she couldn't fault the packed schedule Gabe had arranged for her, sometimes it felt as if she were spending time with a tour guide. Sometimes he was so...*distant*. So...*forbidding*. She would ask him questions designed to understand him better. And he would find a million ways not to answer them. He would change the subject and ask her about growing up in Qurhah. And although he seemed genuinely interested in her life as a princess, sometimes he made her feel as if she was a brand new project he was determined to get right.

He remained as enigmatic as he'd done right from the very beginning. She had married a man who kept his thoughts and feelings concealed and inevitably, that made anxiety start to bubble away beneath the glossy surface of her new life.

It was only during sex that she ever felt on the brink of a closeness which constantly eluded her. When he was making love he sometimes looked down at her, his face raw with passion and his eyes flaring with pewter fire. She wanted him to tell her what it was that kept him so firmly locked away from her. She wanted to look within his heart and see what secrets it revealed. But as soon as his orgasm racked his powerful body, she could sense him distancing himself again.

Oh, he would hold her tightly and bury his lips against her damp skin and tell her that she was amazing. Once he even told her that she was the best lover he'd ever had. But to Leila, his words seemed empty and she was scared to believe them. As if he was saying them because he knew he ought to say them, rather than because he meant them.

She would lie there hugging her still-trembling body while he went off to take a shower, forcing herself to remember that she was only here because of the life growing inside her. A life so new that sometimes it didn't seem as if it were real…

One morning they were lying amid a tumble of sex-scented sheets after a long and satisfying night of lovemaking, when she rolled onto her stomach and looked at him.

'You know, you've never even told me how you made your fortune.'

He stretched out his lean, tanned body and yawned. 'It's a dull story.'

'Every story has a point of interest.'

He looked at her. 'Why do you ask so many questions, Leila? You're always digging, aren't you?'

She met his cool gaze. 'Maybe I wouldn't keep asking if you actually tried answering some of them for a change.'

She could see the wariness in his eyes, but for once she refused to be silenced or seduced into changing the subject. Even if their marriage wasn't 'real' in the way that Sara and Suleiman's was—didn't her position as his wife give her some kind of right to know? To find out whether, beneath that cool facade, Gabe Steel had a few vulnerabilities of his own?

'So tell me,' she murmured and dropped a kiss on his bare shoulder. 'Go on.'

Gabe sighed as he felt her soft lips brushing against his skin. He had never planned to marry her. He hadn't wanted to marry her. Reluctantly, he had taken what

he considered to be the best course of action in circumstances which could have ruined her. He had done
the right thing by her. Yet instead of showing her
gratitude by melting quietly into the background and
making herself as unobtrusive as possible, she had
proved a major form of distraction in ways he had
never anticipated.

From the moment she opened her eyes in the morning to the moment those long black lashes fluttered
to a close at night, she mesmerised him in all kinds
of ways.

The way she rose naked from the rumpled sheets—
a tall, striking Venus with caramel skin and endless
legs. The reverse-heart swing of her naked bottom as
she wiggled it out of the room. The way she slanted
him that blue-eyed look, which instantly had his blood
boiling with lust.

But he knew that women often mistook a man's
lust for love; and that lust always faded. In the normal
scheme of things, that wouldn't matter, but with Leila
it did. He couldn't afford to let her fall in love with
him and have the all too predictable angry outcome
when she realised it wasn't ever going to be recipro-
cated. He didn't want to hurt her. He didn't want her
to start thinking that he could feel things, like other
men did. She was the mother of his child and she
wasn't going anywhere. He might not have wanted to
become a father, but he was going to make damned
sure that this baby was an enduring part of his life.
Which he guessed was why he found himself saying,
'What exactly do you want to know?'

'Tell me how you first got into advertising,' she
said. 'Surely that's not too difficult.'

'Look it up on the internet,' he said.

'I already have.' She remembered how she'd checked him out before that fateful meeting in Simdahab. 'And although there's lots of stuff about you winning awards and riding motorbikes and being pictured with some of the world's most beautiful women—there's not much in the way of background. Almost as if somebody had been controlling how much information was getting out there.' She stroked her finger down his cheek. 'Is that down to you, Gabe?'

'Of course it is.' His response was economical. 'I'm sure your brother controls information about himself all the time.'

'Ah, but my brother is a sultan who rules an empire and has a lot of enemies. What's your excuse?'

She saw the flicker of irritation which crossed his face—a slightly more exaggerated irritation than the look she'd seen yesterday when he'd discovered a dirty coffee cup sitting on the side of his pristine bathtub and acted as if it were an unexploded bomb.

'My excuse is that I try to remain as private as possible,' he said. 'But I can see that you're not going to let up until you're satisfied. Where shall I begin?'

'Were you born rich?'

'Quite the opposite. Dirt poor, as they say—though I doubt whether someone like you has any comprehension of what that really means.'

His accusation rankled almost as much as his attitude, and Leila couldn't hide her hurt. 'You think because I was born in a palace that I'm stupid? That I have no idea what the vast majority of the world is like? I'm surprised at you, Gabe—leaping to stereotypical judgements like that.'

'Ah, but I'm an advertising man,' he said, a smile curving the edges of his mouth. 'And that's what we do.'

'I think I can work out what *dirt poor* means. I'm just interested to know how you went from that to…' the sweeping gesture of her hand encompassed the vast dimensions of the dining room, with its expensive view of the river '…well, *this*.'

'Fate. Luck. Timing.' He shrugged. 'A mixture of all three.'

'Which as usual tells me precisely nothing.'

He levered himself up against the pillows, his gaze briefly resting on the hard outline of her nipples. He felt the automatic hardening of his groin, wondering if that sudden flare of colour over her cheeks meant that she'd noticed it, too.

'I left school early,' he said. 'I was sixteen, with no qualifications to speak of, so I moved to London and got a job in a big hotel. I started in the kitchens—' He fixed her with a mocking look as he saw her eyes widen. 'Does it shock my princess to realise that her husband was once a kitchen hand?'

'What shocks this particular princess is your unbelievable arrogance,' she said quietly, 'but I'm enjoying the story so much that I'm prepared to overlook it. Do continue.'

She saw another brief flicker of sexual excitement in his eyes, but quickly she dragged the cotton sheet up to cover her breasts. She didn't want him seducing her into silence with his kisses.

'I didn't stay in the kitchens very long,' he said. 'I gravitated to the bar where the buzz was better and the tips were good. A big crowd of guys from a nearby advertising agency used to come in for drinks every Friday night—and they used to fascinate me.'

She stared at him. 'Because?'

For a moment, Gabe didn't answer because it was a long time since he'd thought about those days and those men. He remembered the ease with which they'd slipped credit cards from the pockets of their bespoke suits. He remembered their artful haircuts and the year-round tans which spoke of winter sun—at a time in his life when he'd never even had a foreign holiday.

'I wanted to be like them,' he said, in as candid an admission as he'd ever made to anyone. 'It seemed more like fun than work—and I felt I was owed a little fun. They would sit around and brainstorm and angst if they were short of creative ideas. They didn't really notice me hanging around and listening. They used to talk as if I wasn't there.' And hadn't it been that invisibility which had spurred him on—even more than his determination to break free from the poverty and heartbreak which had ended his childhood so abruptly? The sense that they had treated him like a nothing and he'd wanted to be someone.

'They had a deadline looming and a slogan for a shampoo ad which still hadn't been written,' he continued. 'I made a suggestion—and I remember that they looked at me as if I'd just fallen to earth. Some teenage boy with cheap shoes telling them what they should write. But it was a good suggestion. Actually, it was a brilliant suggestion—and they made me a cash offer to use it. The TV campaign went ahead using my splash line, the product flew off the shelves and they offered me a job.'

He remembered how surprised they'd been when he

had coolly negotiated the terms of his contract, instead of snatching at their offer, which was what they'd clearly expected. They'd told him that his youth and his inexperience gave him no room for negotiation, but still he hadn't given way. He had recognised that he had a talent and that much was non-negotiable. It had been his first and most important lesson in bargaining—to acknowledge his own self-worth. And they had signed, as he had known all along they would do.

'Then what happened?'

Gabe shrugged as her soft words floated into his head and tangled themselves up with his memories. He had often wondered about the particular mix of ingredients which had combined to make him such a spectacular success, yet the reasons were quite simple.

He was good with words and good with clients. A childhood spent honing the art of subterfuge had served him well in the business he had chosen. His rise to the top had been made with almost seamless ease. His prediction that digital technology was the way forward had proved unerringly correct. He had formed his own small company and before long a much bigger agency had wanted to buy his expertise. He had expanded and prospered. He'd discovered that wealth begot wealth. And that being rich changed nothing. That you were still the same person underneath, with the same dark and heavy heart.

'I just happened to be in the right place at the right time,' he said dismissively, because thoughts of the past inevitably brought with them pain. And he tried not to do pain. Didn't he sometimes feel that he'd bitten off his allotted quota of the stuff, all in one large and unpalatable chunk? He gave her a long, cool look.

'So if the interrogation is over, Leila, you might like to think about what you want to do today.'

Leila stiffened, her enjoyment of his story stifled by the sudden closure in his voice. Was this what all men did with women? she wondered as she swung her legs over the side of the bed and grabbed a tiny T-shirt and a pair of panties. Tell them just enough to keep them satisfied, but nothing more than that? Keep them at arm's length unless they were making love to them?

But she *knew* all this, didn't she? None of these facts should have surprised her. She'd seen the way her father had treated her mother. She'd seen how quickly women became expendable once their initial allure had worn off. So why the hell was she grasping at rainbows which didn't exist?

She tugged on the T-shirt and pulled on her panties before walking towards the window, suddenly unenthusiastic about the day ahead.

'Why don't you surprise me?' she said flatly. 'Since you're the man with all the ideas.'

She didn't hear the footfall of his bare feet straight away. She didn't even realise he was following her until his shadow fell over her and she turned round to meet the tight mask of his face. She could see the smoulder of sexual hunger in his eyes, but she could see the dark flicker of something else, too.

'What kind of surprise do you want, Leila?'

She could feel the beat of sexual tension as it thrummed in the air around them. He was angry with her for probing, she realised—and his anger was manifesting itself in hot waves of sexual desire. She told herself that she should walk away from him and that might make him realise that sometimes he treated her more like an object than a person. But she couldn't walk away. She didn't want to. And didn't they both want exactly the same thing? The only thing in which they were truly compatible…

She met the smoulder of his gaze and let the tip of her tongue slide along her bottom lip. 'If I tell you then it won't be a surprise, will it?'

'My, how quickly you've learnt to flirt,' he observed softly, his eyes following the movement hypnotically. 'My little Qurhahian virgin hasn't retained much of her innocence, has she?'

'I sincerely hope not,' she returned, 'because a wife who lacks sexual adventure will quickly lose her allure. The women of the harem learn that to their peril.'

Her assertion seemed to surprise him, for his eyes narrowed in response. His gaze drifted down to where the tiny T-shirt strained over her aching nipples.

'You are dressed for sex,' he said huskily.

She tilted her chin. 'I'm hardly dressed at all.'

'Precisely.'

He took a step towards her and backed her into the sitting room towards the L-shaped sofa which dominated one side of the room, and Leila felt excited by the dark look on his face, which made him appear almost *savage*.

She could feel the leather of the sofa sticking to her bare thighs as he pushed her down on it, and her heart began to hammer in anticipation.

'Gabe?' she said, because now he was kneeling on the ground in front of her and pulling her panties all the way down.

But he didn't answer. He was too busy parting her

knees and moving his head between them and, although this was not the first time he had done this, it had never felt quite so intense before.

'Gabe,' she said again, more breathlessly this time as his tongue began to slide its way up towards the molten ache between her legs.

'Shut up,' he said roughly.

But his harsh words were not matched by the exquisite lightness of his touch, and she couldn't help the gasp of pleasure which was torn from her lips. Her eyelids fluttered to a close as she felt the silkiness of his hair brushing against her thighs. Her lips dried as the tip of his tongue flickered against her heated flesh and she groaned.

She felt helpless beneath him—and for a moment the feeling was so intense that she felt a sudden jolt of fear. She tried to wriggle away but he wouldn't let her. He was imprisoning her hips with the grasp of his hands while he worked some kind of sweet torture with his tongue. And surely if she wanted him to stop, she shouldn't be urging him on by uttering his name. Nor clutching at his shoulders with greedy and frantic hands.

She could feel her orgasm building and then suddenly it happened violently, almost without warning. Her fingers dug into his hair as she began to buck beneath him and just when it should have been over, it wasn't over at all.

Because Gabe was climbing on top of her and straddling her—entering her with one hard, slick stroke which seemed to impale her. Gabe was moving inside her, and she was crying out his name again and tears were trickling down her cheeks—and what on earth was *that* all about? She wiped them away before he could see them.

Automatically, she clung to him as he shuddered inside her, his golden-dark head coming to rest on her shoulder and his ragged breath warm against her skin. She found herself thinking that one of life's paradoxes was that intense pleasure always made you aware of your own capacity for intense pain. And wasn't that what had scared her? The certainty that pain was lurking just around the corner and she wasn't sure why.

She closed her eyes and it seemed a long while before he spoke, and when he did his words were muffled against her neck.

'I suppose you're now going to demand some sort of apology.'

She turned her head to face him. She saw his thick lashes flutter open and caught a glimpse of the darkness which still lingered in his eyes. 'I'm not sure that making a woman moan with pleasure warrants an apology,' she said.

His face tightened as he withdrew from her and rolled onto his back, staring up at the ceiling and the dancing light which was reflected back from the river outside. He gave a heavy sigh. 'Maybe it does if that pleasure comes from anger. Or if sex becomes a demonstration of power, rather than desire.'

She didn't need to ask what had made him angry because she knew. Her questions had irritated a man who liked to keep his past hidden. A man who recoiled from real intimacy in the same way that people snatched their hands away from the lick of a flame and she still didn't know why.

Maybe she should just accept that she was wasting her time. Leila's hand crept to her still-flat stom-ach. Shouldn't she be thinking about her baby's needs and the practicalities of her current life, rather than trying to get close to a man who was determined not to let her?

But something made her reach out her hand and to lay it softly over the thud of his heart. 'Well, whatever your motivation was, we both enjoyed it—unless I'm very much mistaken.'

At this he turned his head, and his grey eyes were thoughtful as he studied her. 'Sometimes you sur-prise me, Leila.'

'Do I?'

'More frequently than I would ever have antici-pated.' He stroked his hand over the curve of her hips. 'You know, we ought to think what you're going to do next week.'

'Next week?' She drew her head back and looked at him. 'Why—what's happening next week?'

'I'm going back to work. Remember?' He kissed the curve of her jaw. 'Honeymoons don't last for ever and I do have to work to pay the bills, you know.'

Suddenly she felt unsettled. Displaced. 'And in the meantime, I'm going to be here on my own all day,' she said slowly.

His grey eyes were suddenly watchful. 'Not nec-essarily. I can speak to some of my directors, if you like. Introduce you to their wives so you can get to know them. Some of them work outside the home, but plenty of them are around during the day—some with young children.'

Her heart suddenly heavy, Leila nodded. She didn't want to seem ungrateful and, yes, it would be good to meet women whose company she might soon welcome once her own baby arrived.

But Gabe's words made her feel like an irrelevance. As if she had no real identity of her own. Someone's daughter. Someone's sister and, now, someone's wife.

Well, she *did* exist as a relevant person in her own right and maybe she needed to show Gabe that—as well as to prove it to herself. Back in Qurhah, she had yearned for both personal and professional freedom and surely this was her golden opportunity to grab them.

'I don't want to just kill time while I wait for the baby to be born,' she said. 'I want a job.'

His eyes narrowed. 'A job?'

'Oh, come on, Gabe. Don't look so shocked. Wasn't that what I wanted the first time I ever met you?' She lifted her hand and touched the dark-gold of his hair. 'You thought my photos were good when I first showed them to you. You told me so—and I'd like to think you meant it. Wouldn't your company have work for someone with talent?'

'No,' he said.

Flat refusal was something Leila was used to, but it was no less infuriating when it was delivered so emphatically by her husband. She felt the hot rush of rebellion in her veins. 'I'm not asking you to pull any strings for me,' she said fiercely. 'Just show my work to someone in your company—anonymously, of course—and let them be the judge.'

'No,' he said again.

'You can't keep saying no!'

'I can say any damned thing I please. You're asking *me* for a job, Leila—remember? And I'm telling you that you can't have one. That's the way it works when you're an employer.'

She stared at him mulishly and thought that, at times, Gabe's attitude could be as severe as her brother's. 'Why not?' she demanded. 'I'd like to know exactly what it is you're objecting to. The accusations of nepotism, which won't stand up if I get the job on my own merits? Or is it something else—something you're not telling me?'

Gabe got off the sofa and began to walk towards the bedroom, shaking his head as if denying her question consideration. She thought that he was going to leave the room without answering when he suddenly turned back and it was only then that she realised that he was completely naked. And completely aroused. Again.

'It's your proximity I'm having a problem with,' he declared heatedly, wondering how she managed to get under his skin time and time again. 'I'll have to be with you the whole damned time, won't I? In the car. In the canteen—'

'Standing by the water cooler?' Her mouth twitched. 'Or does some minion bring you water on a silver tray in a crystal glass?'

'We're talking about my life—not yours, princess!' he iced back. 'And how can someone judge your work when you don't have it? You haven't even brought your portfolio with you, have you? You left it in Qurhah.'

'Yes, I did. But I have all the images on a USB stick,' she said sweetly. 'So that won't be a problem.'

Gabe made a stifled sound of fury as he walked away towards the bathroom, wishing for the first time ever that he had a door to slam. But he had chosen the apartment because there *were* no doors. Because one room flowed straight into the next, each characterised by a disproportionate amount of light and space. He had chosen it because it was the antithesis of the places he'd inhabited during his childhood—and now the very determined Princess Leila Scheherazade was making him want to lock himself away. She was invading his space even more than she had already done. And there didn't seem to be a damned thing he could do to stop it.

He would have someone show her portfolio to Alastair McDavid—at Zeitgeist's in-house photographic studio. And he would just have to hope that Alastair found her work *good*—if not quite good enough.

He turned on the shower and his mouth hardened as the punishing jets of icy water began to rain down on him. Because something told him that his hopes were futile and that Leila would soon have her exquisite foot in yet another door.

CHAPTER NINE

THE PANORAMIC VIEW outside his penthouse office gave him a moment's respite before Gabe refocused his gaze on the woman who was sitting at the other side of his desk.

Of course his hopes had been futile. And *of course* Leila got the job she'd secretly been lusting after. Leaning back in his swivel chair, he looked into the excited sparkle of his wife's blue eyes. Though maybe that was an understatement. She hadn't just 'got' the job, she had walked it—completely winning over Alastair McDavid, who had described her photos as 'breathtaking' and had suggested to Gabe that they employ her as soon as possible.

Gabe drummed his fingertips on the polished surface of his desk and attempted to speak to her in the same tone he would use to any other employee. But it wasn't easy. The trouble was that he'd never wanted to kiss another employee before. Or to lock the door and remove her clothes as quickly as possible. The X-rated fantasies which were running through his mind were very distracting, and his mouth felt as dry as city pavement in the summer. 'At work, I am your boss,' he said coolly. 'Not your husband or your lover. And I don't want you ever to forget that.'

'I won't.'

'While you are here, you will have nothing to do with the Qurhah campaign.'

'But—'

'No buts, Leila. I'm telling you no—and I mean it. It will only complicate matters. People working on the account might feel inhibited dealing with you—a woman who just happens to be a princess of the principality. Their creativity could be inhibited and that is something I won't tolerate.' He subjected her to a steady look, glad of the large and inhibiting space between them. 'Is that clear?'

'If you say so.'

'I do say so. And—barring some sort of emergency—you will not come to my office again unless you are invited to do so. While you are here at Zeitgeist, you will receive no deferential treatment—not from me, nor from anyone else. You are simply one of the four hundred people I employ. Got that?'

'I think I'm getting the general idea, Gabe.'

Gabe couldn't fail to notice the sardonic note in her voice, just as he couldn't fail to notice the small smile of triumph she was trying to bite back, having got her way as he had guessed all along she would. And maybe he should just try to be more accepting about the way things had turned out. Alastair McDavid was no fool—and he'd said that Leila had an extraordinarily good eye and that her photos were pretty near perfect. Her talent was in no doubt—and, since her work had been submitted anonymously, nobody could accuse him of nepotism.

But Gabe was feeling uncomfortable on all kinds of levels. For the first time ever his personal life had entered the workplace and he didn't like it. He didn't like it one bit. Despite years of occasional temptation and countless invitations, he'd never dated an employee or a client before. He had seen for himself the dangers inherent in that. There had never been some hapless female sobbing her eyes out in the women's washroom because of something *he'd* done. He'd never been subjected to awkward silences when he walked into boardroom meetings, or one of the Zeitgeist dining rooms.

The less people knew about him, the better, and he had worked hard to keep it that way. He was never anything less than professional with his workforce, even though he joined in with 'dress-down Friday' every week and drank champagne in the basement bar next door whenever a new deal was signed. People called him Gabe and, although he was friendly with everyone from the janitor to the company directors, he maintained that crucial personal distance.

But Leila was different.

She looked different.

She sounded different.

She was distracting—not just to him but to any other man with a pulse, it seemed. He had driven her to work this morning—her first morning—and witnessed the almost comical reaction of one of his directors. The man had been so busy staring at her that he had almost driven his car straight into a wall.

Her endless legs had been encased in denim as she'd climbed out of Gabe's low sports car, with one thick, ebony plait dangling down over one shoulder.

In her blue shirt and jeans, she was dressed no differently from any of his other employees, yet she had an indefinable head-turning quality which marked her out from everyone else. Was that because she'd been brought up as a princess? Because she had royal blood from an ancient dynasty pulsing through her veins, which gave her an innate and almost haughty bearing? When he looked at her, didn't he feel a thrill of something like pride to think that such a woman as this was carrying his child? Hadn't he lain there in bed last night just watching her while she slept, thinking how tender she could be, and didn't he sometimes find himself wanting to kiss her for absolutely no reason?

Yet he knew those kinds of thoughts were fraught with danger. They tempted him into blotting out the bitter truth. They ran the risk of allowing himself to believe that he was capable of the same emotions as other men. And he was not.

He frowned, still having difficulty getting his head round the fact that she was sitting in *his* office as if she had every right to be there. 'Anything you want to ask *me*?' he questioned, picking up a pencil and drawing an explosion of small stars on the 'ideas' notepad he always kept open on his desk.

'Do people know I'm pregnant?'

He looked up and narrowed his eyes. 'Why would they?'

'Of course. Why would they?' she repeated, and he thought he heard a trace of indignation in her voice. 'Heaven forbid that you might have told somebody.'

'You think that this is something I should boast about, Leila? That an obviously unplanned pregnancy has resulted in an old-fashioned shotgun marriage?

It hasn't exactly sent my reputation shooting up into the stratosphere.' He gave a dry laugh. 'Up until now, I'd always done a fairly good job of exhibiting fore-thought and control.'

Pushing back her chair, she stood up, her face suddenly paling beneath the glow of her olive skin. 'You b-bastard,' she whispered. 'You complete and utter bastard.

He'd never heard her use a profanity before. And he'd never seen a look of such unbridled rage on her face before. In an instant he was also on his feet. 'That didn't come out the way it was supposed to.'

'And how was it *supposed to* come out?' She bit her lip. 'You mean you didn't intend to make me sound like some desperate woman determined to get her hooks into you?'

'I was just pointing out that usually I don't mix my personal life with my business life,' he said, raking his fingers through his hair in frustration.

'I think you've made that abundantly clear,' said Leila. 'So if you've finished with your unique take on character assassination cunningly designed as a pep talk, perhaps I could go and start work?'

For once Gabe felt wrong-footed. He saw the hurt look on her face and the stupid thing was that he wanted to kiss her. He wanted to break every one of his own rules and pull her into his arms. He wanted to lose himself in her, the way he always lost himself whenever they made love. But he fought the feeling, telling himself that emotional dependence was a luxury he couldn't afford. He knew that. He knew there were some things in life you could never rely on and that was one of them.

But guilt nagged at him as he saw the stony expression on her face as she turned and walked towards the door. 'Leila?'

She turned around. 'What?'

'I shouldn't have said that.'

Her smile was wry. 'But you did say it, Gabe. That's the trouble. You did.'

Shutting his office door behind her, Leila was still simmering as she walked into the adjoining office to find Alice waiting for her and with an effort she forced herself to calm down. Because what she was *not* going to do was crumble. She could be strong—she knew that. And she needed to be strong—because she was starting to realise that she couldn't rely on Gabe to be there for her.

Oh, he might have put a ring on her finger and made her his wife, but she couldn't quite rid herself of the nagging doubt that this marriage would endure—baby or not.

Pushing her troubled thoughts away, she smiled at Alice. 'Gabe says you're to show me around the Zeitgeist building,' she said. 'Though judging by the size of it, I think I might need a compass to find my way around the place.'

Alice laughed. 'Oh, you'll soon get used to it. Come on, I'll show you the canteen first—that's probably the most important bit. And after that, I'll take you down to the photographic studios.'

Leila quickly learnt that paid employment had all kinds of advantages, the main one being that it didn't give you much opportunity to mope around yearning for what you didn't have.

Overnight, her first real job had begun and, although she was fulfilling a lifetime ambition just by *having* a job, she found it a bit of a shock. She'd grown up in a culture which encompassed both opulence and denial, but she had never set foot in the workplace before. She was unprepared for the sheer exhaustion of being on her feet all day and for being woken by the alarm clock every morning. Quickly, she discovered that dressing at leisure was very different from having to be ready to start work in the studio at eight-thirty. Her lazy honeymoon mornings of slow lovemaking were replaced by frantic clockwatching as she rushed for the shower and grappled with her long hair.

'You don't have to do this, you know,' said Gabe one morning as they sat at some red lights with Leila hastily applying a sweep of mascara to her long lashes.

'What? Wear make-up?'

'Very funny. I'm talking about putting yourself through this ridiculous—'

'Ridiculous what?' she interrupted calmly. 'Attempt to prove that I'm just like everyone else and that I need some sense of purpose in my life? Shock! Horror! Woman goes out to work and wears make-up!'

'What does the doctor say about it?' he growled.

'She's very pleased with my progress,' Leila answered, sliding her mascara back into her handbag. 'And it may surprise you to know that the majority of women work right up until thirty-six weeks.'

She sat back and stared out of the car window, watching the slow progress of the early-morning traffic. Gabe's car was attracting glances, the way it always did. She guessed that, when viewed from the outside, her life looked like the ultimate success story.

As if she 'had it all'. The great job. The gorgeous man. Even a little baby on the way.

From the inside, of course—it was nothing like that. Sometimes she felt as if her marriage was as illusory as the many successful advertising campaigns which Gabe's company had produced. Those ones which depicted the perfect family everyone lusted after with the artfully messy table with Mum and Dad and two children sitting around it, giggling.

Yet everyone at Zeitgeist knew that the model father in the advert was probably gay and that the model mum's supposedly natural beauty was enhanced by hair extensions and breast implants.

No, nothing was ever as it seemed.

Nothing.

Gabe was still Gabe. Compelling, charismatic but ultimately as distant as a lone island viewed from the shoreline. And she realised that was the way he liked it. The way he wanted to keep it. They weren't growing closer, she realised. If anything, they were drifting further apart.

One evening, they arrived back at the apartment after an early dinner out and Gabe went straight to their bedroom to change. Minutes later he reappeared in jeans and a T-shirt, with his face looking like thunder.

'What the hell has been going on?' he demanded. 'Have we been burgled?'

Leila walked over to where he stood, looking at the room behind him with a sinking heart. He had left early for a meeting this morning and somehow she'd slept through the alarm and had woken up really late. Which meant that she had left home in a rush, and it showed—particularly as today was the cleaner's day off.

Automatically, she moved forward and started to pick up some of the discarded clothes which lay like confetti all over the floor. A pair of knickers were lying on his laptop. 'I overslept,' she said, hastily grabbing them from the shiny surface. 'Sorry.'

Her words did nothing to wipe the dark expression from his face, for tonight he seemed to be on some kind of mission to get at her. 'But it isn't just when you oversleep, is it, Leila?' he demanded. 'It's every damned day. I keep finding used coffee cups around the place and apple cores which you forget to throw away. Did nobody ever teach you to tidy up after yourself, or were there always servants scurrying around to pick up after you?'

Leila flinched at the cold accusation ringing from his voice, but how could she possibly justify her general untidiness when his words were true?

'I did have servants, yes.'

'Well, you don't have servants now, and I value my privacy far too much to want any staff moving in—not even when the baby's born. So if we're to carry on living like this, then you're really going to have to learn to start being more tidy.'

The words leapt out at her like sparks from a spitting fire.

If we're to carry on living like this.

Biting her lip, she turned away, but Gabe caught hold of her arm and pulled her against him.

'I'm sorry.'

'It doesn't matter.'

'It does. That came out too harshly. Sometimes I

just…snap,' he said, his head lowering as he made to brush his lips over hers.

But Leila pushed him away. He thought that making love could cure everything—and usually it did. It was always easy to let him kiss her, because his kisses were so amazing that she always succumbed to them immediately. And when she was in his arms he didn't feel quite so remote. When he was deep inside her body, she could allow herself to pretend that everything was just perfect. Yet surely that was like just papering over a widening crack in the wall, instead of addressing the real problem beneath.

Sometimes she felt as if she was being a coward. A coward who was too scared to come out and ask him whether he wanted her out of his life. Too scared that he might say yes.

She went into the bathroom and showered, and when she emerged in a cotton dress which was beginning to feel snug against her expanding waist, it was to find him sipping at a cup of espresso.

He looked up as she entered the room, and suddenly his grey eyes were cool and assessing.

'I have a deal coming up which means that I need to go to the States,' he said. 'Will you be okay here on your own?'

'Of course,' she said brightly, but, coming in the wake of their recent spat, his words sounded ominous.

She walked over to the fridge and poured herself a glass of fizzy water, exaggeratedly wiping the few spilt drops from the work surface before going to perch on one of the bar stools.

'How long will you be gone?' she asked.

'Only a few days.'

Gabe saw the tremble of her lips, which she couldn't quite disguise, and suddenly the coffee in his mouth seemed to taste sour. Yet he knew exactly what he was doing. He was insightful enough to know that he was pushing her away, but astute enough to know that he could offer her no other option. Because the thought of getting close to her was making him *feel* stuff. And that was something he didn't do.

He put down his coffee cup with more force than he intended.

If only it could be different.

His mouth hardened as he stared into the bright blue of her eyes.

It could never be different.

That night they lay on opposite sides of the bed, the heavy silence indicating that neither was asleep, though neither of them spoke. His sleep was fractured, his disturbing dreams forgotten on waking—leaving him with a heavy headache which he couldn't seem to shift.

He was just sliding his cell phone into his jacket pocket when he walked into the sitting room to find Leila looking at his passport, which he'd left lying on the table.

'That's a very sombre photo,' she commented.

'You aren't supposed to smile in passport photos.'

Leila found herself thinking that he wouldn't have much of a problem with that. That unless the situation demanded it, his natural demeanour was unsmiling. Those chiselled cheekbones and cold eyes lent themselves perfectly to an implacable facade.

She glanced down at his birth date and her heart

gave a funny little twist as she glanced back up at him. 'Will you phone me?'

'Of course.' He took the passport from her and brushed his mouth over hers in a brief farewell kiss. 'And I'll be back on Sunday. Keep safe.'

But after he'd gone, all the energy seemed to drain from her. Leila sat down on the sofa and stared into space, her heart thumping like someone who had just run up an entire flight of stairs without stopping. The date on his passport was March fifteenth—the Ides of March. She knew that date. Of course she did. Wasn't it etched firmly in her mind as heralding the biggest change in her life?

She shook her head, telling herself not to be so stupid. It was a coincidence. Of course it was.

Over the next few days, she was grateful to be able to lose herself in the distraction of work—glad that its busy structure gave her little time to dwell on the uncomfortable thoughts which were building like storm clouds in her mind. Alastair McDavid announced that Zeitgeist had just landed a big contract to advertise a nationwide chain of luxury hotels and spas. And since spa clientele consisted mainly of women, it was in everyone's interest to use a female photographer.

'And we'd like to use you, Leila,' he told her with a smile.

Leila was determined not to let him down and the excitement of planning her first solo assignment was almost enough to quell the disquiet which was still niggling away inside her. Almost, but not quite.

Sunday arrived and Gabe texted to say that he was just about to catch his plane. She wished she was in a position to collect him from the airport, but she still hadn't learnt to drive. She had allowed her husband and his chauffeur to ferry her everywhere. It had been all too easy to lean on Gabe—and if she wasn't careful that could get to be a lasting habit.

Because for the first time she was beginning to acknowledge the very real fear that this marriage seemed destined to fail.

She remembered his cold rebuke about her general untidiness, yet she hadn't even factored in what the presence of a tiny baby was going to do to Gabe Steel's ordered existence. What if he hated having a screaming infant in his slick, urban apartment? Wouldn't he get irritated if she went off sex, as she'd been told that new mothers sometimes did?

Her distraction grew as she showered and washed her hair, then picked out a long tunic dress in palest blue silk, which she'd brought with her from Qurhah. She didn't question why she had chosen to wear that particular tunic on that particular day. All she knew was that it covered her body from neck to ankle and she wondered if she was seeking comfort in the familiar.

She pinned her hair into a simple up do and made tea while she tried not to feel as if she was waiting. But she *was* waiting. Waiting for some sort of answer to a question she wasn't sure she wanted to ask.

What was it that they said in Qurhah? That if you disturbed a nest of vipers, then you should expect to get bitten.

She heard the click of the front door opening and the sound of Gabe closing it again. He didn't call her name, but his footsteps echoed on the polished wooden floor as they approached, and her heart began to race as he walked into the room.

For a moment he stood very still and then he came over and kissed her, but she pulled away.

'How's Leila?' he questioned, his eyes narrowing as they stared into her face.

'I'm fine,' she said brightly. 'Shall I make some coffee?'

'I had some on the plane. Any more coffee and I'll be wired for a week.' He glanced down at the stack of unopened mail which was waiting for him before looking up again. 'So what's been happening while I've been away?'

'My...scan went well,' she said carefully, her fingers beginning to pleat at the filmy blue fabric of her tunic. 'And I have some good news. Alastair wants me to do the assignment for the new spa contract.'

'Good.'

She looked up from her fretful pleating and suddenly her throat felt so dry that she could barely get the words out. 'And March fifteenth is your birthday.'

He gave a short laugh. 'Interesting that you should tell me in an almost accusatory manner something I've known all my life.'

She told herself not to be intimidated by the coldness in his voice, nor to freeze beneath the challenge icing from his pewter eyes. 'That's the day we had... sex in Simdahab.'

'And?' His dark eyebrows elevated into two sardonic arcs. 'Aren't I allowed to have sex on my birthday?'

She shook her head. She was still a relative novice when it came to lovemaking, but she was intuitive enough to know that something about him that afternoon had been different. Something she hadn't seen since. There had been something *wild* about his behaviour that day. Something seeking and restless. She chose her words carefully. 'You gave me the distinct impression that having spontaneous sex with someone you'd only just met wasn't your usual style.'

'Maybe you were just too irresistible.'

'Is that true?'

Gabe met the steady stare of her bright blue eyes and, inwardly, he cursed. If she was a casual girlfriend, he would have told her it was none of her business, and then to get out and leave him alone. But Leila was his wife. He couldn't tell her to get out. *And the truth was that he didn't want to.*

He met her eyes. 'No, it's not true,' he said quietly. 'I seduced you that day because I was in Qurhah, a place where it's almost impossible to buy whisky, which is my usual choice of drink on my birthday.' There was a pause. 'And in the absence of the oblivion brought about by alcohol, I opted instead for sex.'

CHAPTER TEN

LEILA STARED INTO eyes as flat as an icy sea as Gabe's words hit her. Her fingernails were digging into the palms of her hands but she barely noticed the physical discomfort—not when this terrible pain was lancing through her heart and making it almost impossible for her to breathe. 'You used me?' she questioned at last. 'Because you couldn't get a drink?'

His laugh was bitter. 'There's no need to be quite so melodramatic about it. People have sex for all kinds of reasons, Leila. Sometimes it's because lust just gets the better of them and sometimes because it makes them forget.' He threw his passport down on the table and looked at her. 'I didn't use you any more than you used me that day. I wanted oblivion and you wanted to experiment. Am I right?'

Leila squirmed beneath the challenge of his gaze because his words were uncomfortably close to the bone. How could she deny his accusation when it was true? She *had* wanted to experiment, yes—but she'd had her reasons. What would he say if she told him that he had seemed to represent everything a man should be? Everything that she'd ever dreamed of.

That for the first time in her life, she'd actually *believed* all those romantic films she'd been hooked on.

Yet, in a way, maybe that had been seeking her own kind of oblivion. She had found pleasure with a devastatingly handsome and sexy man—and for a few brief moments she had forgotten the prison of her palace life. But she hadn't really known him as *Gabe*, had she?

She still didn't.

'What were you seeking to obliterate?' she asked carefully.

'It isn't relevant.'

'Oh, I think it is.' She sucked in a breath and held his gaze as she let it out again. 'Look, I get it,' she said. 'I get that you're a very private man who doesn't want to talk about emotions.'

'So don't ask me.'

She shook her head as she ignored the cold clamp of his words. 'But I *have* to ask you—don't you see? I know all the psychology books say that yesterday is gone. But I don't want to go on like this—not knowing stuff. I'm having your baby, Gabe. Don't you think that gives me the right to know something about your past, as well as the occasional speculation about what our future might hold?'

With an angry shake of his head, Gabe walked over to the window to stare out at one of the most expensive views in the world. It was ironic, he thought. You could buy yourself somewhere high in the sky, which was far away from the madding crowd. But no matter how much you spent or how much you tried to control your life—you could never keep the world completely at bay. You could only try. He could feel the hard beat of his heart as he turned round to face her.

'It isn't relevant,' he said again.

'It *is*,' she argued. 'We can't just keep burying our heads in the sand and pretending this isn't happening, because it is. We're going to have a baby, Gabe. A baby which needs to be cared for. Not just cared for. Loved,' she said, her voice faltering a little.

'Don't look to me for love, Leila,' he said tonelessly. 'I thought I'd made that clear from the beginning.'

'Oh, you did. You made it very clear, and I wouldn't dream of expecting you to love *me*,' she said. 'But surely our baby has the right to expect it. If you can't show our baby love—and believe me when I tell you I'm not judging you if that's the case—then don't I at least have the right to know why?'

For a moment there was silence while Gabe looked at the set of her shoulders and the steady blue gaze which didn't falter beneath his own deliberately forbidding stare. He knew what she wanted. What women always wanted. To find out why he didn't show emotion or even feel it. It was something he'd come up against time and time again—and women were the most tenacious of creatures. Countless numbers had tried—and failed—to work him out. Powerful women, rich women, successful women—they all wanted the one thing which eluded them. They saw his cold heart as a challenge; his emotional isolation as something they wished to triumph over.

Yet Leila's question had not been tinged with ambition—rather with the simple desire to understand. She was the mother of their baby and maybe what she said was true. Maybe she *did* have the right to know what had made him the person he was. But wasn't he scared to let her close? Scared of what might happen if he did?

He surveyed her from between half-shuttered eyes. 'What do you want me to tell you?'

Leila was so surprised at his sudden change of heart that it took a moment before she could speak, and all the time her head was telling her to go easy. Not to scare him off with a fierce interrogation.

'Oh, I don't know,' she said softly. 'All the usual things. Like, where you were born. I don't even know that.'

For a moment, there was silence. It reminded her of the moment before the start of a play, when the whole theatre was quiet and prepared for revelation. And then he began to speak.

'I was born in the south of France. But we moved back to England when I was a baby—to a place called Brighton.'

'Yes, Brighton. I've heard of it.' Leila nodded and began reciting, as if she were reading from a geographical textbook. 'It's a seaside town on the south coast. Is it very beautiful—this Brighton?'

In spite of everything, Gabe gave a glimmer of a smile. At times she seemed so foreign and so *naive* but of course, in many ways, she was. Maybe she thought he came from a background like hers and telling her that he had been born on the French Riviera would only feed into that fantasy.

The truth, he reminded himself. She needed to know the truth.

'Anywhere by the sea has the potential to be beautiful,' he said. 'But, like any town, there are rough parts—and those were the places we lived. Not that we stayed anywhere very long.'

'We?'

'My mother and me.'

'Your father wasn't around?'

Gabe could taste the sudden bitterness in his mouth. He wanted to stop this unwanted interrogation right now, but he realised that these questions were never going to go away unless he answered them.

And wasn't it time he told *someone*?

'No, my father wasn't around,' he said. 'He and my mother split up before I was born. Things ended badly and she brought me back to England, but she had no family of her own and no money. When she met my father, she'd been working as a waitress—and that was all she was qualified to do.'

'So, was your father French?' questioned Leila, thinking that he didn't look French.

He shook his head. 'No. He was Russian.'

Slowly, she nodded, because that made sense. Much more sense. The high, chiselled cheekbones, which made his face look so autocratic and proud. The icy grey eyes. The hair, which looked like dark, molten gold. 'So what kind of childhood did you have?' she asked quietly.

He shrugged, as if it didn't matter. 'It was largely characterised by subterfuge. My mother was always afraid that my father would try to find me and so we were always on the move. Always living just below the radar. Our life was spent running. And hiding.'

If he thought about it, he could still remember the constant sensation of fear. Of looking over his shoulder. Of being told never to give anything away to any stranger he might meet. He had quickly learnt how to appear impenetrable to those he met.

And hadn't the surveillance and masquerade skills he'd acquired stood him in good stead for his future career? He had discovered that the world of advertising was the world of illusion. That what you saw was never quite what you got. The masks he had perfected to keep his identity hidden had been invaluable in his role as a powerful executive. They were what had provided him with his chameleon-like reputation. As careers went, his background had been a perfect fit.

'My mother took what jobs she could,' he said. 'But it was difficult to juggle poorly paid work around childcare and I pretty much brought myself up. I soon learnt to look after myself. To rewire dodgy electrics and to shop for cheap food when the supermarkets were about to close.'

Leila blinked in surprise, because the image he painted was about as far away from the sophisticated billionaire she'd married as it was possible to imagine. But she still thought there was something he wasn't telling her. Some dark secret which was lurking just out of sight. *I need to know this for my baby*, she thought fiercely. *For* our *baby*.

'And?'

His mouth hardened. She saw the flash of something bleak in the depths of his eyes before it was gone again.

'I used to feel indignant that my father had never bothered to look us up. I wondered why he didn't seem to care how his son was doing—or why he'd never once offered to help out financially. It became something of an obsession with me. I used to ask my mother what he was like, but she never wanted to talk about him. And the more she refused to tell me, the more frustrating I found it.'

His words tailed off, and for a moment he said nothing. Leila held her breath but didn't speak, not wanting to break his concentration.

'As I grew older, I became more determined to find out something about him,' he continued. 'I didn't necessarily want to be with him—I just wanted to *know*.'

'Of course you did,' she said.

Their eyes met, and Gabe suddenly got a painful flash of insight. Maybe he'd wanted to know for exactly the same reasons that Leila wanted to know about *him*. Maybe everybody had a fundamental desire to learn about their roots. Or the roots of the child they carried...

'But my mother was scared,' he said. 'I can see that now. She was scared that I would run to a man she feared. That I would choose him over her.' He gave a bitter laugh. 'Of course, I only discovered this afterwards.'

'Afterwards?' she echoed as some grim ending glinted as darkly as thick blotting paper held over the beam of a flashlight.

He nodded, and the way he swallowed made Leila think of barbed wire; of something jagged and sharp lodging in his throat and making his words sound painful and distorted.

'It was the eve of my sixteenth birthday,' he said. 'We were living in this tiny hole of place. It was small and dark and I started wondering what kind of life my father had. Whether he was wealthy. Or whether he was reduced to eating food which was past its sell-by date and shivering like us, because it was the coldest spring in nearly thirty years. So I asked my mother the same question I'd been asking ever since I could remember. Did she have any idea where he was or what he did? And as always, she told me no.'

'And you believed her?' questioned Leila tentatively.

He shrugged. 'I didn't know what to believe, but I was on the brink of adulthood and I couldn't tolerate being fobbed off with evasive answers any more. I told her that the best birthday present she could give me would be to tell me the truth. That either she provided me with some simple facts about my parentage—or I would go and seek my father out myself. And that she should be under no illusion that I would find him. I was probably *harsher* than I should have been, but I had the arrogance of youth and the certainty that what I was doing was right.'

There was complete silence, and Leila's heart pounded painfully as she looked at him, for she had never seen an expression on a man's face like that before. Not even when her brother had returned from that terrible battle with insurgents in Port D'Leo and his two most senior commanders had been slain in front of him. There was a helplessness and a hopelessness glinting in Gabe's eyes which was almost unbearable to observe.

'She said she would tell me the next day, on my birthday. But…'

His words tailed off and Leila knew he didn't want to tell her any more, but she needed to know. *And he needed to say it.* 'But what?'

'I think she meant to tell me,' he said. 'But I also

think she was terrified of the repercussions. Afraid that she might lose me.' His mouth twisted. 'But when I got back from school the next day, she couldn't tell me anything at all because she was dead.'

Leila's heart lurched as she stared at him in alarm, not quite believing what he'd just said. *'Dead?'*

For a long moment, there was silence. 'At first I thought she was just sleeping. I remember thinking that I'd never seen her looking quite so peaceful. And then I saw…I saw the empty pill bottle on the floor.'

Leila's throat constricted as she struggled to say something, imagining the sight which must have greeted the young boy as he arrived home from school. She stared at him in utter disbelief. 'She… *killed herself*?'

'Yes,' he said flatly.

Leila felt a terrible sadness wrap itself around her heart. She had wanted to understand more about Gabe Steel and now she did—but she had never imagined this bleak bitterness at the very heart of his life. She could hardly begin to imagine what it must have been like for him. So that was why he had locked it all away, out of sight. That was why he kept himself apart—why he deliberately put distance between himself and other people.

She was stunned by what he had told her. Yet out of his terrible secret came a sudden growing sense of understanding. No longer did it surprise her that he didn't want to trust or depend on women—because hadn't the most important woman in his life left him?

And lied to him.

'Did you blame yourself?' she asked quietly.

'What do you think?' he bit out, his icy facade now completely shattered.

She saw emotion breaking through—real, raw emotion—and it was so rare that instinctively she went to him and he didn't push her away. He let her hold him. She wrapped her arms around him and hugged him tightly and she could feel his heart beating hard against her breast. Pressing her lips against his ear, she whispered, 'You mustn't blame yourself, Gabe.'

'No?' He pushed her away, like somebody who had learned never to trust words of comfort. 'If I hadn't been so persistent…if I hadn't been so damned stubborn—then my mother wouldn't have felt driven to commit such a desperate act. If I hadn't been so determined to find out about my *father*, she need never have died. She could have lived a contented old age and been cushioned by the wealth I was to acquire, but which she never got to see.'

For a moment Leila didn't answer, wondering if she dared even try. Because how could someone like her possibly empathise with Gabe's rootless childhood and its tragic termination? How could she begin to understand the depths of grief he must have experienced when he was barely out of boyhood? That experience had formed him and, emotionally, it had warped him.

Up until that moment, Leila had often thought herself hard done by. Her parents' marriage had been awful—everyone at court had known that. Her father had spent most of his time with his harem, while her mother had sat at home heartbroken—too distracted to focus on her only daughter. As if to compensate for that, Leila had been pampered and protected by her royal status but she had felt trapped by it too. She had been isolated and lost during a childhood almost as lonely as Gabe's.

But his circumstances had been different. He had been left completely on his own. He had lived with his guilt for so long that it had become part of him. 'Your mother must have been desperate to have taken such a drastic action,' she said quietly.

His voice was sardonic. 'I imagine she must have been.'

She stumbled on. 'And she wouldn't want you to carry on blaming yourself.'

'If you say so, Leila.'

She swallowed, because one final piece of the jigsaw was missing. 'And did you ever find your father? Did you track him down?'

There was a heartbeat of a pause before his mouth hardened. 'No.'

'Gabe—'

'No.' He shook his head. 'That's enough. No more questions, Leila. And no more platitudes either. Aren't you satisfied now?'

His eyes were blazing, and she wondered if she'd gone too far. If she'd pushed him to a point where he was likely to break. She wondered if he was going to walk out. To put distance between them, so that when they came face to face again he could pretend that this conversation had never happened.

But he didn't do any of that. Instead, he pulled her back into his arms. He stared down at her for a long moment before bending his head to kiss her—the fiercest kiss she could ever have imagined. She knew what he was doing. He was channelling his hurt and his anger and his pain into sex, because that was what he did. That was how he coped with the heavy burden he carried.

Leila clung to him, kissing him back with all the passion she was capable of, because she wanted him just as much. But she wanted so much more than just sex. She ached to give him succour and comfort. She wanted to show him that she was here for him and that she would always be here for him if only he would let her. She would warm his cold and damaged heart with the power of her love. Yes, love. She loved this cold, stubborn husband of hers, no matter how much he tried to withdraw from her.

'Gabe,' she whispered. 'My darling, darling Gabe.'

The breath he let out in response was ragged and that vulnerable sound only added to her determination to show him gentleness. Her hand flew up to the side of his face and, softly, she caressed his jaw. Did her touch soothe him? Was that why his eyelids fluttered to a close, as if he was unspeakably weary? She touched those too, her fingertips whispering tenderly over the lids, the way she had done all that time ago in Simdahab.

Beneath the tiptoeing of her fingers, his powerful body shuddered—shaking like a mighty tree which had been buffeted by a major storm. He opened his eyes and looked at her but there was no ice in his grey eyes now. Only heat and fire.

He picked her up and carried her over to the sofa, and she'd barely made contact with the soft leather before he was impatiently rucking up her filmy blue dress and sliding down her panties. His hand was shaking as he struggled with his own zip, tugging down his trousers with a frustrated little moan.

She was wet and ready for him and there were few preliminaries. But Leila didn't want them; she just wanted Gabe inside her. His fingers parted her slick, moist folds and she gasped as he entered her, closing her eyes as he filled her.

'Gabe,' she said indistinctly, but he didn't answer as he began to move.

It was fast and deep and elemental. It seemed to be about need as much as desire, and Leila found herself responding to him on every level. Whatever he demanded of her, she matched—but she had never kissed him quite as fervently as she did right then.

Afterwards, she collapsed against the heap of the battered cushions, her heart beating erratically as she made shallow little gasps for breath. She turned to look at him, but he had fallen into a deep sleep.

For a while she lay there, just watching the steady rise and fall of his chest. She thought about what he had told her and she flinched with pain as she took her mind back to his terrible story. He had known such darkness and bleakness, but that period of his life was over. He had taken all the secrets from his heart and revealed them to her—and she must not fail him now.

Because Gabe needed to be loved; properly loved. And she could do that. She could definitely do that. She would care for him deeply, but carefully—for fear that this bruised and damaged man might turn away from the full force of her emotions.

She must love him because he needed to be loved and not because she demanded something in return. She might wish for that, but it was not hers to demand.

She snuggled closer, feeling the jut of his hip against her belly. She ran her lips over the roughness of his jaw and then kissed the lobe of his ear as she wrapped her arms tightly around his waist.

'I will love you, Gabe Steel,' she whispered.

But Gabe only stirred restlessly in his sleep.

CHAPTER ELEVEN

THE DISTANT RUMBLE of thunder echoed Leila's troubled thoughts.

Had she thought it would be easy? That Gabe's icy heart would melt simply because he'd revealed all the bitter secrets he'd carried around with him for so long? That he'd instantly morph into the caring, sharing man she longed for him to be?

Maybe she had.

She glanced out of the window. Outside, the tame English skies were brewing what looked like the fiercest storm she had witnessed since she'd been here. Angry grey clouds billowed up behind St Paul's Cathedral and the river was the colour of dark slate.

She had tried to reassure herself with the knowledge that, on the surface, things in their marriage were good. Better than before. She kept telling herself that, as if to accentuate the positive. Gabe was teaching her card games and how to cook eggs, and she was learning to be tidier. He massaged her shoulders at the end of a working day and they'd started going for country walks on the weekend. Her pregnancy was progressing well and she had passed the crucial twelve weeks without incident. Her doctor had told her that she was blooming—and physically she had never felt better.

Her job, too, was more fulfilling than she could ever have anticipated. At first, Leila had suspected that most of the staff at Zeitgeist had been wary of the boss's wife being given a plum role as a photographer, but none of that wariness had lasted. According to Alastair, her outlook was fresh; her approach original—and she got along well with people.

Her photos for the spa campaign had confounded expectation—the expectation being that it was impossible to get an interesting shot of a woman wrapped in a towel.

But somehow Leila had pulled it off. Maybe it was the angle she had used, or the fact that her background had equipped her to understand that a woman didn't have to show lots of flesh in order to look alluring.

'And anyway,' she had said to Gabe as they were driving home from work one evening, 'these spas are trying to appeal to a female audience, not a male one. Which means that we don't always have to portray women with the not-so-subtle subtext that they're constantly thinking about sex.'

'Unlike you, you mean?' he had offered drily.

She had smiled.

Yes, on the surface things were very good.

So why did she feel as if something was missing— as if there was still a great gaping hole in her life which she couldn't fill? Was it because after that awful disclosure about his mother, Gabe had never really let down his guard again? Or because her expectations of a relationship were far more demanding than she'd realised? That she had been lying to herself about not wanting his love in return, when it was pretty obvious that deep down she craved it.

There were moments which gave her hope—when she felt as if they were poised on the brink of a new understanding. When she felt as close to him as it was possible to feel and her heart was filled with joy. Like the other day, when they had been lying in bed, she'd been wrapped in his arms and he'd been kissing the top of her head and the air had felt full of lazy contentment.

But then she'd realised that for the first time she could feel the distinct swell of her belly, even though she was horizontal at the time.

With an excited little squeal, she'd caught hold of his hand and moved it to her stomach. 'Gabe. Feel,' she'd whispered. 'Go on. Feel.'

She knew her husband well enough to realise that he would never give away his true feelings by doing something as obvious as snatching his hand away from her skin, as if he'd just been burned. But she felt his whole body tense as he made the most cursory of explorations, before disentangling himself from her embrace and telling her that he had to make an international call.

So what was going on beneath the surface of that cold and enigmatic face? Leila gave a sigh. She didn't know. You could show a man love, but love only went so far. Love couldn't penetrate brick walls if people were determined to erect them around their hearts. Love could only help heal a person if that person would allow themselves to be healed.

Gabe made her feel as if she'd wrested every secret from him and that he found any more attempts at soul-searching a bore. Maybe she just had to accept that this was as good as it got. That the real intimacy she longed for simply wasn't going to happen.

But that didn't mean she was going to stop loving him.

She turned away from the thundery skyline to where he was lying sprawled out on the leather sofa, and her heart gave a little twist.

She could never stop loving him.

'Gabe?'

'Mmm?'

'I was wondering if we could give a party?'

He looked up and frowned. 'What kind of party?'

'Oh, you know—something revolutionary. Invite some people along, give them food and drink, maybe play a little music. That sort of thing.'

'Very funny.' Stretching his arms above his head, he gave a lazy yawn. 'What exactly did you have in mind?'

She drew in a deep breath. 'Well, we've never really had a wedding party, have we? I mean, we had that lunch with Sara and Suleiman, but that was all. And I've become quite friendly with Alice and a few of the others from work, so I'd quite like to invite them. And then there's my brother. I'd quite like to see him.' She wriggled her shoulders. 'I'd just like a bit of a celebration before the baby comes. Some kind of acknowledgement that the wedding actually happened.'

He didn't answer straight away.

'As long as it's not here,' he said eventually. 'But if you want to hire a hotel or a restaurant, then that's fine by me.'

'Oh, Gabe,' she said, and walked back across the

room to hug him and when she stopped hugging him she could see that he was actually *smiling*.

Leila threw herself into a frenzy of organisation. She booked the award-winning wedding room at the Granchester Hotel and hired a party planner who came highly recommended by Alice.

The party's colour scheme of gold and indigo was chosen to reflect the colours of the Qurhahian flag and the cuisine was intended to offer delicacies from both cultures. A group of barber-shop singers had been booked for a cabaret spot at ten and dozens of fragrant crimson roses were on order.

Responses soon came flooding in. Everyone at Zeitgeist who'd been invited said yes. Sara and Suleiman were going to be there and also Sara's brother. Even Murat accepted his invitation, much to Leila's pleasure and surprise. It seemed that everybody wanted to attend the wedding celebration of a desert princess and a man known for never giving parties. Leila bought a new dress for the occasion—a gorgeous shimmery thing with threads of silver running through a grey silky material, which reminded her of the mercurial hue of Gabe's eyes.

She took off the day before the party but Gabe was tied up with wall-to-wall meetings all morning.

He was frowning as he kissed her goodbye. 'I'll meet you for lunch,' he said. 'And for goodness' sake—calm down, Leila. You're wearing yourself out with this damned party.'

Something in his tone had made her tilt her head back to look at him. 'You do *want* this party, don't you?'

For a moment there was silence and his smile was

faintly rueful as he shook his head. 'I never said I wanted it, did I? I agreed to it because it makes you happy.'

She stared at the door as it closed behind him.

Wanting to make her happy was a step forward, she guessed—even if it made her feel a bit like a child who needed to be placated with a new toy. Like a spoilt little princess who'd stamped her foot and demanded a party. The same spoilt princess who had finally remembered to throw away her apple cores and to remember that there wasn't a squad of servants poised to tidy up after her.

In an effort to subdue her sudden feeling of restlessness, she decided to try a little displacement therapy. Walking over to the concealed wardrobe, she pulled out her new skyscraper grey heels, which were jostling for room with the rest of her shoes. She really was going to have to ask Gabe to give her more cupboard space, since she had far more clothes than he did. Or maybe she should just do the sensible thing and acquire some for herself.

She practised walking around the bedroom in her new shoes and decided that they didn't hurt a bit. Then she jigged around a little and decided they would be fine to dance in. And in spite of all her reservations, she felt a soaring sense of excitement to think that she might get to dance with her husband for the first time ever.

Pulling open one of the wardrobe doors which Gabe rarely used, she was relieved to find it almost empty. She could shift some of her clothes in here. She took off her shoes and bent down to place them neatly on the rack at the bottom, when she noticed the corner of a drawer protruding, spoiling the otherwise perfect symmetry of the wardrobe's sleek interior.

She wondered what drew her eyes to the manila colour of an envelope inside, but it was enough to make her hesitate. Was that why she didn't immediately push the drawer shut, but slowly open it as curiosity got the better of her?

She didn't know why her heart was beating so fast, only that it was. And she didn't know why her husband should have wedged an envelope in some random drawer when he kept all his paperwork in the bureau in his study next door. Fingers trembling, she flipped open the top of the envelope because she could see that inside there were photos. Photos of a man. A stranger, yet…

Her heart missed a beat as she pulled out another photo. This time there were two men and one she recognised instantly because it was Gabe. But of course she recognised the other man too, because his features were unmistakeable.

High, slashed cheekbones. Piercing pewter eyes and dark golden hair. She swallowed. Two men standing outside what looked like a Parisian café. One of them her husband and the other very obviously his father.

But Gabe had never met his father! He'd told her that. She remembered the way his mouth had tightened and the bitter look which had darkened his eyes as he'd said it.

The envelope slipping from her fingers, Leila slid to her knees. He *had* met his father. There was photographic evidence of it right in front of her eyes. He had told her that this marriage would be based on truth, but it seemed that it was based on nothing but a tissue of lies.

Lies.

She felt the acrid taste of bile rising up in her throat and in that moment she felt utter defeat, wondering how she could have been so blind. So *stupid.* They didn't have love, no matter how much she wanted it— and now it seemed that they didn't even have trust either.

But she had ignored all the signs. She had blithely done what women were so good at doing. She had refused to listen to all the things he'd told her, because it hadn't suited her to listen. He'd told her that he didn't do love but she had thought—arrogantly, it seemed now—that she might just be able to change his mind.

And in that showy-off way, she had decided to throw a party which he clearly had no appetite for— *he'd even told her that, too.* She was planning to dress up in her new, shimmery party frock and her slightly too-high grey shoes and to explode into the flower-decked wedding room of the Granchester and make as if it were all okay. As if she were just like every other bride—happy and contented and expecting a baby. But she wasn't, was she?

Maybe she could have been that bride. Maybe she could have settled for sex and affection and companionship, without the magic ingredient of love. She knew that plenty of people were happy enough with that kind of arrangement. But not lies. Because lies were addictive, weren't they? You told one and you might as well tell a million.

The walls felt as if they were closing in on her, even

though they were made of glass. But claustrophobia was all in the mind, wasn't it? Just like trust.

She scrabbled around and found a sweater and pulled it on, because suddenly she was shivering. Shivering as if she'd caught a violent bout of flu. She grabbed her handbag and took the elevator downstairs and the porter she'd seen on her wedding day was there.

She rarely saw him these days, because usually she was rushing past with Gabe, or because they took the elevator straight down to the underground car park. It was as much as she could do to flash him a smile, but something on her face must have alarmed him for he rose to his feet, a look of concern on his face.

'Everything all right, Mrs Steel?'

The unfamiliar use of her married name startled her but, with an effort, Leila pinned a smile to her face. 'I'm fine. I just want some fresh air.'

'Are you sure? Looks like rain,' he said doubtfully.

Yes. And it felt like rain, too. Inside her heart, it felt as if the storm had already broken.

She started walking; she didn't know where. Somewhere. Anywhere. She didn't really pay attention to the route she was taking. She wasn't used to the streets of London, but she didn't care. A reckless gloom came over her. Maybe it was best that she got used to these streets now, so that when she was living on her own she would have a better idea of the geography of the city.

The rain began to fall. Slowly at first and then harder and more relentlessly, but Leila barely felt it, even though after a few minutes she was soaked right through. During the gaps between the loud thunderclaps above her, she could hear her phone vibrating in her handbag, but she ignored it.

She walked and walked until the riverbank became unfamiliar and the houses and shops less glitzy and much closer together. She saw people with angry dogs straining at their leashes. She saw youths huddled in shop doorways sheltering from the rain, dragging cigarette smoke deep into their lungs.

She didn't know how long she'd been walking when she found a café. Her wet hair hung in stringy rat's tails as she sat dripping in a steamy corner and ordered a mug of strong tea. Her phone began to ring and, uninterestedly, she pulled it out. She saw that it was Alice and that she had four missed calls—three of them from Gabe.

She pressed the answer button. 'Hello.'

'Leila, is that you?' Alice sounded frantic.

'Yep. It's me.'

'Are you okay? Gabe's been going out of his mind with worry. He says he hasn't been able to get hold of you.'

Leila stared at the steam which rose from her mug like smoke from a bonfire. 'I'm fine,' she said tiredly. 'I just needed some fresh air.'

'Leila.' Alice's voice now dipped to soft and cautious. 'Where *are* you?'

'It doesn't matter.'

'It does. You sound…strange. Let me send a car for you.'

'No.'

'Then at least tell me where you are,' pleaded Alice. 'Just to put my mind at rest.'

Wearily, Leila looked down at the laminated menu

and gave the name of the café. She would leave before Alice had a chance to send anyone, which was clearly what she had in mind. But her feet were aching and she was cold. Like, really cold. As if somebody had taken her bones and turned them into ice. So she just sat there as the minutes ticked away and the chatter of the other customers seemed to be taking place in a parallel universe.

She felt hungry, too. Hungry in a way which was unfamiliar to her and she knew that this was the baby speaking to her. Finding herself unable to ignore the unfamiliar cravings of her body, she ordered a white bread sandwich stuffed with thick slices of cheese and smothered in a sharp and pungent brown chutney.

She fell on it with an instinctive greed which seemed beyond her control and that was how Gabe found her. He walked into the humble café, his face sombre and his dark golden hair so wet that it looked almost black. Raindrops were running down over the high slash of his cheekbones and for one crazy moment it looked almost as if he were crying.

But Gabe didn't do tears, she reminded herself. Gabe didn't do emotions because he didn't *feel*. Gabe's hurt and pain had made him immune from the stuff which afflicted normal human hearts, like hers.

He walked straight over to her and leant over the table. Holding on to the back of a chair, he seemed to be having difficulty controlling his breathing and it was a moment before he could ice out his incredulous question.

'What the hell do you think you're doing, Leila?'

'What does it look like I'm doing? I'm eating a cheese and pickle sandwich.' She finished chewing a mouthful which now tasted like sawdust and stared at him. 'Anyway, I thought you were in meetings.'

'I cancelled them when I didn't hear from you. I've been going out of my mind with worry.'

'So Alice said.'

'So Alice said,' he repeated, and then his eyes narrowed. 'Don't you *care*?'

At this, she put the rest of the sandwich down on the plate but her hands were still trembling as she met the accusation in his eyes.

'Don't I *care*?' She gave a short laugh. 'I did. I cared very much. But I realise now how incredibly stupid I've been. I mean, how could I possibly think that ours was a marriage worth saving? You told me that our relationship was to be based on truth and you lied. A loveless marriage I could just about live with, but not lies, Gabe. Not lies.'

And with that, she pushed back her chair and ran out of the café.

CHAPTER TWELVE

THE COOL RAIN hit Leila's face as she met the fresh air, but Gabe was hot on her heels. She ran straight past the chauffeur-driven car which was obviously his, but he caught up with her before she'd reached the end of the street.

His hands on her elbows, he hauled her round to face him and held on to her tightly, even though she tried to struggle out of his grip.

'You can't run away,' he said grimly.

'I can do anything I like. And I want to be as far away from you as possible. So go away and leave me alone.'

'I'm not going anywhere without you and I'm not having this discussion in the middle of the street in the pouring rain.'

'Terrified it will ruin your ice-cool image?' she mocked.

'Terrified that you'll catch a cold—especially in your present condition,' he said. 'You're pregnant, Leila. Remember?'

'*Oh!*' She gave a howl of frustrated rage as she struggled again. 'As if I could ever forget!'

But he was levering her gently towards the waiting

car, and the chauffeur had leapt out to open the door.
Gabe was easing her onto the back seat and Leila was
appalled at how relieved she felt as warmth and luxury wrapped themselves round her body like a soft
and comforting mantle.

That's just the external stuff, she reminded herself
bitterly. *Money just makes things more comfortable.
It doesn't change anything. It doesn't make the hurt
and betrayal go away.*

She turned to face him as he slid onto the seat beside her. 'I'm not going back to your apartment!'

'We don't have to do that,' he said evenly. 'Where
would you like to go instead?'

And wasn't that the saddest thing of all—that
she couldn't think of anywhere? The place she most
wanted to be was in his heart, and there was no place
for her there.

'I don't care,' she said.

'Then let's just drive around for a while, shall we?
And you can tell me what's wrong.'

'What's wrong? *What's wrong?*' She hated the way
he was talking to her as if she were aged a hundred
and had forgotten where she lived. It was as much as
she could do not to bang her fists frustratedly against
his chest. And sudden all her hurt and pain and disappointment came bubbling out. 'I'll tell you what's
wrong! You told me that our marriage was to be based
on truth. You told me you couldn't promise me love,
but you could promise me that. And I believed you.'
Tears sprang from her eyes and began to trickle down
her cheeks. 'I believed you even though I wanted the
impossible from you. I wanted your love, but I was
prepared to settle for the truth.'

'Leila—'

'And then this morning.' Angrily, she shook away the hand which he'd placed on her arm. 'This morning I found some photos stuffed away in a drawer in the wardrobe.'

He went very still. 'So you've been spying on me, have you?'

'Don't you dare try to turn this on me! I was actually looking for a bigger home for my shoe collection—but that's not the point! The point is that I found photos of you with a man who was clearly your father. A man you told me you'd never met. You lied to me, Gabe. You *lied to me.*'

There was silence in the car, punctuated only by the muffled sound of her sobs and, reluctantly, she took the handkerchief he withdrew from his pocket and buried her nose in it.

'Yes, I lied to you,' he said heavily. 'I lied to you because...'

His voice faded away and it was so unlike Gabe to hesitate that Leila lifted her nose from the handkerchief to look at him. Her vision was blurred through her tears but she saw enough to startle her, for his eyes looked like two empty holes in a face so ravaged with emotion that for a moment he didn't look like Gabe at all.

'Because, what?'

He shook his head and turned to her as the words began to spill from his lips, as if he'd been bottling them up for a long time. 'What if you were a man and you met a woman who just blew you away, in a way you didn't recognise at the time—because it had never happened to you before? Maybe you were determined not to recognise it because it was something you didn't believe in. Something which, deep down, you feared.'

Leila sniffed. 'None of that makes sense.'

'Hear me out.' He sucked in a deep breath. 'So you walk away from this woman, telling yourself that you've made the best and the only decision you could possibly make. But you're not sure. In fact, you're starting to realise that you've just done the dumbest thing imaginable, when she turns up at your home in London. And you look at her and realise what an idiot you've been. You realise that here you have a chance for happiness right in front of your eyes, but you're scared. And then...'

His voice tailed off and she saw his features harden.

'Then?'

'Then she tells you she's pregnant and you're even more scared. Because this is a double-edged sword. On the one hand, it means you can be together legitimately without having to delve too deeply into your own emotions. Yet on the other...'

'Gabe!' Her anger forgotten now, she leaned forward—wondering what on earth could have put such a haunted expression on his face. 'Will you please stop talking in riddles? The fact is that you lied about seeing your father and nothing can change that.'

'No. Nothing can change that. But what if I told you there was a reason why my mother kept his identity from me?' He raked his fingers back through his plastered hair and his fingertips came away wet. For a moment he just stared at them, as if he might find some kind of answer gleaming back at him from that damp, cold skin.

'After she died, I felt angry and bitter—and guilty

too. But I went to London and I started working and, as I told you, success came pretty quickly.'

'Yes,' she said quietly. 'You told me.'

'I embraced my new role as a successful business-man but sometimes—not often—I would think about my father. I couldn't eradicate the curiosity which still niggled away at me. I didn't know if he was dead or alive. I wanted to confront him. I wanted to know why he'd abdicated all his responsibilities towards me. I wanted to tell him that a woman had died sooner than reveal his identity.' He clenched his fist, as if he wanted to hit something. Or someone. 'I guess I was looking for someone to blame for her death. Some-one who wasn't me.'

'Go on,' she said.

'I was rich by this point. Rich enough to find any-one I wanted and it didn't take long to track my fa-ther down in Marseilles, which is where he'd moved to when he'd left Provence. And suddenly I under-stood my mother's behaviour. I understood why she'd wanted to protect me from him. Why she'd feared his influence on me…'

His words tailed off as if he couldn't bear to say them but Leila leaned forward, her wet hair falling over her shoulders as she peered into his face. 'What, Gabe? *What?*'

'Which particular title shall I give him? Gangster or hoodlum?' he questioned bitterly. 'Because he an-swered to both. He was an underworld figure, Leila. A powerful and ruthless individual. I discovered that he had killed. Yes, killed. I discovered this when we met in Paris and not long afterwards he was gunned

down in some gangland shootout himself. That photo
was taken by one of his associates and it's the only one
of us together. Time after time I went to burn it, but
something always stopped me and I still don't know
what that something is.'

'Oh, Gabe,' she whispered, her voice distorted with
shock and pain. 'Why the hell didn't you tell me?'

'Because I *couldn't*. Don't you see, Leila?' His eyes
were blazing as his voice cracked with emotion. 'His
blood is my blood. And it's our baby's blood too. How
could I knowingly pass on a legacy like that to you?
How could I possibly tell the sister of the Sultan about
her baby's forebears? Not just a grandmother who had
committed suicide, but a grandfather who was a mur-
derer. How could I subject you to a life of fear that
those tainted genes will have been passed down to
the next generation?' There was silence for a moment
as his eyes burned into hers. 'I'm damaged, darling.
Badly damaged. Now do you understand?'

Leila nodded. Yes, she understood. She understood
this powerful man's pride and fear, but also about
his deep desire to protect. And Gabe had been trying to protect her. From hurt and pain and worry. He
had been trying to protect their baby too—from the
heartache and fear that evil might be inherited, like
blue eyes or the ability to draw.

He wanted to reach out to her, but he didn't know
how.

She looked into his haunted face and her heart went
out to him, but she knew that this was her golden opportunity and that she must not shrink from it. She had

wanted to be his equal, hadn't she? And she wanted to be strong.

So show him that you're still there for him. Love him the way you really want to love him. Why let him shoulder this burden on his own, when you're more than willing to share it with him?

Her voice was low and trembling as her words came tumbling out. 'Do you have any idea of the history of Qurhah?' she demanded.

He looked at her as if this was the last thing in the world he had expected her to say. 'I can't see how that is relevant.'

'Can't you? Actually, it's *very* relevant. I'll have you know that my family is descended from mighty warriors and ruthless tyrants. There have been Al-Maisan sultans conquering neighbouring lands ever since our people first settled in the desert, and there has been much bloodshed along the way. Nobody's history is whiter than white, Gabe. Not yours and especially not mine.'

He shook his head. 'That's not the same,' he said stubbornly.

She laid her hand on his arm. 'It *is* the same—just different. Our baby isn't a clone of your father, you know. Nor of you—or me. Our baby is unique and I know for sure that the best and only legacy we can give him—or her—is love. We must love this baby with all our hearts, Gabe. Even if you don't feel that way about me—do you think you can find it in your heart to love our baby?'

He shook his head and for a minute his face was contorted with pain. 'What a brute of a man you must think I am,' he declared bitterly, 'that I would be incapable of feeling something for an innocent scrap of humanity.'

'Not a brute,' she said gently. 'A man who has been wounded—badly wounded. But I am your wife and I am going to help you heal, but I can only do that if you let me. If you can bear to open up your heart, Gabe—and let me in.'

She saw a muscle flickering at his temple as he caught hold of her wet shoulders and looked into her face.

'Only if you can you forgive me,' he said. 'Can you ever forgive me for what I have done, my darling Leila?'

'There's nothing to forgive,' she said softly, her hand reaching up to touch the hard contours of his face. She ran her fingertip along the high slash of his very Slavic cheekbones and the firm curve of his lips. She looked into the pewter eyes and her heart turned over with love. One day soon she would tell him to learn to understand his father, and then to let the bitterness go. That there was a little bit of bad in the best of people, and a little bit of good in the worst.

But not now.

Now she must be focused on the most important things.

'We're both very cold and very wet,' she said as she snuggled up against him. 'Do you think we should go home?'

Gabe stroked a straggly strand of damp hair away from her face and smiled, but the lump in his throat meant that it took a moment or two before he could speak. 'Right here is home,' he said unevenly. 'Wher-

ever you are. I love you, my compassionate and passionate princess. I love you very much.'

He tapped on the glass and the car moved away,
and that was when he started to kiss her.

EPILOGUE

'HE LOOKS VERY Qurhahian,' said Gabe as he gazed into the crib where the sleeping infant lay.

Leila smiled, giving one last unnecessary twitch of the snowy cashmere blanket which now covered the crescent curve of Hafez's perfect little foot. 'Do you know, that's exactly what Murat said to me today.'

'Did he?'

She nodded as she looked down at their tiny son. His skin was faintly tinged with olive and already he had a hint of the slightly too-strong nose which had been the bane of her life, but which Gabe always told her was the most beautiful nose in the world. Deep down she suspected that her husband was relieved to discover that their firstborn looked more like her than him. But Leila was confident that, with time, his few remaining reservations about his heritage would melt beneath the power of her love.

Today had been Hafez's naming ceremony, here in the palace in Simdahab where she'd grown up—and it had been the most glorious of visits. All the servants had clucked excitedly around the princess's new baby. That was when they hadn't been buzzing round the Western guests who had flown out for the occasion and who mingled with the dignitaries and kings from the neighbouring desert countries.

It had been a day of immense happiness and joy, but Leila thought that Murat seemed rather pensive and she wondered if it was because the woman he had been destined to marry had found happiness with another man.

She put her arms around Gabe and pressed her lips to his cheek. 'My brother said something very strange to me today.'

'Tell me.' He started to kiss her neck.

Leila closed her eyes as shivers of sensation began to whisper over her skin. 'He said that at least there was another generation of the Al-Maisan family, in case he never produced an heir of his own. He seemed to imply that he would never marry—and that he'd be contented with a long line of mistresses instead.'

Gabe smiled as he brushed his mouth over her scented skin. Hadn't he once thought that way himself? When his heart had been so dark and cold that it had felt as if a lump of ice had been wedged in his chest. 'All it takes is the right woman,' he said. 'And once she comes along, it seems that a man will happily change his entire life to please her. Just as I have done for you.'

'Oh, darling,' she said, closing her eyes with dreamy pleasure as she thought back to everything that had happened to them since Hafez had been born.

They had sold his apartment and moved to a large house overlooking Hampstead Heath, because Gabe realised that Leila had been right. That his minimalistic high-rise apartment was no place to bring up a baby—it had suited a phase of his life which was now over. Hafez needed grass and flowers, she had told him firmly. He needed a nearby nursery and hopefully a school he could walk to.

So a studio had been built for her in the basement of their new house, from which she would work as a freelance photographer. That way she got all the pleasures of working, but none of the regular commitment which would keep her away from their son.

Gabe lifted his hand and stroked back the glorious fall of hair from her face so that it streamed down over her shoulders in a cascade of ebony. The roseate curves of her lips were an irresistible invitation, and he kissed her with a steadily increasing hunger before drawing away from her.

'I love you,' he said.

'I know. The feeling is shared and returned.'

'And there's a spare hour to fill before the palace banquet,' he said a little unsteadily. 'Shall we go to bed?'

She opened her eyes. 'You're insatiable.'

'I thought you liked me that way.'

'I like you any way I can get you,' she whispered back. 'But preferably without any clothes on and nobody else around.'

'You are a shameless woman, Leila Steel.'

'Lucky that's the way you like *me*,' she teased.

'I know,' he said. 'I never stop reminding myself how lucky I am.'

And this was the greatest of the many truths he'd discovered in a life now lived without pretence, or fear or regret.

Next week was his birthday but he wouldn't be seeking to blot out the past with a bottle of Scotch and oblivion. He would be embracing the golden and glorious present with his wife and their beloved baby son.

And he would be telling Leila how much he loved her, just as he did every single day of his life. His beautiful Qurhahian princess who had brought his heart to life with the power of her love. Just as the rains fed the dormant flower seeds, to bring the desert miracle to the Mekathasinian Sands.

* * * * *

A sneaky peek at next month...

MODERN™

POWER, PASSION AND IRRESISTIBLE TEMPTATION

My wish list for next month's titles...

In stores from 21st February 2014:

❑ A Prize Beyond Jewels – Carole Mortimer

❑ Pretender to the Throne – Maisey Yates

❑ The Sheikh's Last Seduction – Jennie Lucas

❑ The Woman Sent to Tame Him – Victoria Parker

In stores from 7th March 2014:

❑ A Queen for the Taking? – Kate Hewitt

❑ An Exception to His Rule – Lindsay Armstrong

❑ Enthralled by Moretti – Cathy Williams

❑ What a Sicilian Husband Wants – Michelle Smart

Available at WHSmith, Tesco, Asda, Eason, Amazon and Apple

Just can't wait?

Visit us Online

You can buy our books online a month before they hit the shops! **www.millsandboon.co.uk**

0214/01

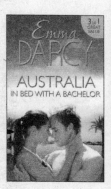

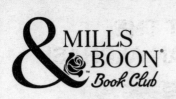 

MILLS & BOON
Book Club

Join the Mills & Boon Book Club

Want to read more **Modern**™ books?
We're offering you **2 more** absolutely **FREE!**

We'll also treat you to these fabulous extras:

- 🌹 Exclusive offers and much more!

- 🌹 FREE home delivery

- 🌹 FREE books and gifts with our special rewards scheme

Get your free books now!

visit www.millsandboon.co.uk/bookclub
or call Customer Relations on 020 8288 2888

Discover more romance at

www.millsandboon.co.uk

- ♥ WIN great prizes in our exclusive competitions
- ♥ BUY new titles before they hit the shops
- ♥ BROWSE new books and REVIEW your favourites
- ♥ SAVE on new books with the Mills & Boon® Bookclub™
- ♥ DISCOVER new authors

PLUS, to chat about your favourite reads, get the latest news and find special offers:

- 🔲 Find us on facebook.com/millsandboon
- 🐦 Follow us on twitter.com/millsandboonuk
- ♥ Sign up to our newsletter at millsandboon.co.uk

WEB_SD